AF409852

This Little Secret

To Rainbow Nutbutter, specifically the cosmic brownie flavor, for pulling me through late night word crunches.

A RECAP OF BOOK ONE IS
COMING UP. DO NOT TURN THE
PAGE IF YOU HAVE NOT READ
BOOK ONE!

ARE YOU SURE YOU READ BOOK ONE?

ALMOST TO THE RECAP.

IF YOU ARE HERE FOR SPOILERS,
I HOPE BOTH SIDES OF YOUR
PILLOW ARE WARM.

RECAP OF THIS LITTLE TOWN
(Book 1: Grove Hills Series)

1. Jorja Bonovich finds out Peter Ellison and Rush True were working together to bring her family down. She also learned that Rush wanted to stop the plans, aborted the mission, but Peter kept it going.

2. Jorja finds out that Toby and Rush both have feelings for her, and she can't deny she feels the same.

3. Jorja finds out her father is not really Jerome Bonovich, but Peter Ellison's dad, Edward Ellison. Jorja's mother slept with Edward as a form of "payment" and orchestrated by her father Jerome. At least, this is what she was led to believe.

4. The book ends with Jorja killing Jerome Bonovich by dissolving sleeping pills into his nightly glass of whiskey. Rush and Toby help Jorja throw the body overboard a boat into the river that surrounds the town of Grove.

CHAPTER ONE

Jorja

My body jolted, and I sat up for what felt like the millionth time, rubbing my eyes and the sweat from my brow. Sleep would elude me forever—I was sure of it. What do people do after they murder someone, anyway? Obviously, they didn't sleep. However, Jerome never had trouble sleeping every night. Maybe because he was used to it, or because he was just *that* horrible of a person it didn't affect him like it did me.

I tossed and turned a few more times before settling on my back and staring at the ceiling, replaying every move Toby, Rush, and I made after disposing of the body. I told them to go home and burn whatever they were wearing, and I put my things into the fireplace at home and made sure they turned to ash.

What if the guys didn't do it? I had a feeling that the what ifs would haunt me forever. I never thought I was capable of something as big as murder. Smart enough to accomplish it? Yes.

His car.

I sat up quickly and started getting dressed. I had to get his vehicle somewhere else. The security cameras outside were recently replaced after they were found to be broken when Peter destroyed my car. I knew how to turn them off but those would be the first thing the investigators would look at once my father's disappearance went viral.

The cameras.

I smacked my forehead. They would have me and the guys dragging the body into the woods. Every inch of my skin broke out in a cold sweat.

After grabbing a pair of winter gloves, I hurried through the house until I got to Jerome's office where the security recordings were. How could one night feel like a thousand hours? I slipped the gloves on before typing in the password on the computer and turning off the security system. I deleted the archived videos from the past twenty-four hours and knew I only had a matter of minutes before the authorities would get an alert that the system had been turned off. After making sure everything was deleted, I promptly turned the system back on, hoping I was fast enough.

I found the car keys and a small canister of pepper spray in Jerome's desk drawer. Grabbing both,

I hurried down the stairs. In the span of thirty seconds, the plan was made to drive his car to the funeral home and walk to Rush and Toby's house from there. It was only four blocks away, and hopefully it'd look like I had snuck out and stayed with them. I felt so confident earlier—that I could actually pull this off—but now, I wasn't so sure.

After pulling into the funeral home parking lot, I parked on the side where the cameras wouldn't have a good view of me. The car would be in view, but it'd be hard to make out who I was. I kept the hood of my hoodie over my head and quickly made my way through the woods to head to the guy's house.

My heart raced, not just from how fast I was walking, but because it felt like someone was following me. I made plans of how I'd fight to get away if someone were close by and decided to attack. Bears were also a concern, but not as scary as who could be waiting for me out there.

Every snap of a twig and whisper of wind sent shivers down my spine. I remembered the pepper spray in my pocket and tightened my grip on it giving me momentary reassurance. I should've grabbed a gun, but those were locked tightly in a safe and would've taken too much time to retrieve. I picked up my pace, doing my best to focus on what was ahead of me instead of what or who could be following me.

Rush's window was locked, and before I ever tried Toby's, a part of me knew his would stay unlocked. Climbing through his window didn't go as gracefully as I had thought it would. His bed was under the window, and falling on top of him definitely wasn't a part of the plan.

I whispered apologetically over and over, trying to shush him as he shouted my name and we both went tumbling out of his bed onto the floor. He hovered over me, the light from his night-light plugged into the wall near his bed illuminating the space around us.

"You have a night-light?"

A strained grin appeared as he peered down at me. His breaths were labored, and his eyes were still wide from shock. "You snuck into my window, woke me up by falling into my bed, and the first thing you say to me is about my night-light?"

"Are you scared of the dark?"

"I like to see where I'm going if I get up in the middle of the night." He moved off me until he was standing and offered me a hand. I took it and stood.

Laughing a little, I said, "So, you *are* scared of the dark."

"Maybe."

I snorted. "No way."

He rubbed the back of his neck and chuckled. "Jorja, I don't think the night-light is as important as the reason you're here. What's going on? Are you alright?"

I pulled Jerome's car keys from my hoodie pocket. I clenched them tight in my fist before slowly opening my hand and revealing them to Toby. I huffed in frustration. I was so sure I had had everything covered, and admitting I hadn't thought it all through was embarrassing.

"Keys?"

I nodded and looked at him. "I don't know what to do with them. I didn't think of everything, Toby. The cameras ... the car ... I walked here ... I don't even know what time it is—"

"Wait, you walked here?"

I nodded, pulling the pepper spray from my pocket. "I have pepper spray." I smiled innocently.

His deep frown was confirmation he still didn't approve.

"I'm fine. Not a scratch." I rolled up my sleeves to prove it and then put the canister of pepper spray back into my pocket.

He sighed heavily. "Your house is so far from here."

"I didn't walk from my house. I walked from the funeral home where I left Jerome's car. I—" My breathing picked up as my mind started to fill with all the possible loose ends and panic started to settle in my chest, the heaviness of it all making it hard to breathe. "I know I said we will never speak of the murder again, but—"

He held his hand out. "Give me the keys."

"But—"

"Give me the keys, Jorja."

I put them into his hand then started chewing on my nails, a habit I had never picked up before tonight.. "I hate that I have you and Rush involved in this mess. It's unfair to the both of you. You can back out at any time. I'll understand and—"

"Jorja?"

I looked up at him.

He put the keys into his other hand and gently moved my hand away from my mouth, holding my hand tightly. "Breathe. I'm involved because I want to be. My brother, too. We are going to get through this. Together."

"I'm supposed to be the strong one. The one who is trained to do this. I was supposed to do a clean job. Everything is ... messy. I didn't think it through."

"Thinking about everything you didn't do isn't going to change that what's done is done. We just move forward from here and be smart about every move we make."

I took a deep breath and let it out. "You're right."

"After I get rid of the keys, what do we need to do next?"

"I deleted the security camera footage for the past twenty-four hours. I can't think of anything else right now."

He nodded as he thought. "How are you going to explain that?"

"I'm hoping they won't ask me questions. That they won't even suspect me." I chewed on the inside of my cheek. "What are you gonna do with the keys?"

"Metal melts," he said calmly.

I nodded. "Good idea." I looked down at my hand he was still holding. When he noticed, he slowly let go.

"I should take you home."

I shook my head. "No, because they can't see your truck on the cameras. I had it planned it would just look like I snuck out to be here with you guys. It'll make sense."

"What about fingerprints?"

"I wore gloves." I looked at the bedroom door. "Is your dad home?"

He shook his head. "He's on call tonight."

"I should go let Rush know I'm here. I'm just telling him I snuck out because I couldn't be in that house alone. The keys, the cameras ... don't tell him. The less that know all the details the better."

"But—"

"Please."

He pressed his lips together and nodded.

"I'm going to let him know I'm here. Thank you, Toby." I hugged him, and the warmth from his bare chest comforted me. "I mean it. Thank you," I whispered.

His fingers moved through my hair and down my back, settling in the middle before holding me tightly against him. "You owe me. Big time." He sighed heavily and let his arms drop to his sides. "Go see Rush. I'll handle these," he said, holding up the keys.

After taking a step back, a soft smile spread across my lips. You'd think covering up a murder would take precedence over my conflicted feelings for Toby, but thoughts of how it would be to allow the curiosity of being with him took over. The thought of Rush quickly interrupted my sudden urge to kiss Tobias True, so I left the room before I could make another lethal mistake tonight.

I made my way down the hall until I found Rush's door. I opened it gently, and unlike Toby's room, his room was pitch black. I used the light from my phone to make my way through all the dirty clothes and shoes on the floor until I made it to his bed. I laid down next to him and rubbed his bare shoulder softly.

"Rush," I whispered.

His eyes fluttered open, and, when he saw me, he smiled. It took less than a second for his smile to fade, and his eyes widened. He sat up quickly. "What's wrong?"

I sat up slowly and hugged one of his pillows to my chest. "I couldn't sleep." That was mostly true. He couldn't know the rest. That was between Toby and me, and it had to stay that way.

"How'd you get in?"

"Toby's window. Yours was locked."

He yawned. "So, he knows you're here?"

I nodded. "He does."

He ran his fingers through his hair, tousled from sleep, and sighed. "You could've just called. I would've let you in the front door."

Shrugging seemed like the best response. Calling would've left a phone trail. Too many clues when the investigation starts. If I started talking, I'd never shut up, and I didn't want to worry Rush with more secrets.

"I know you said we can't ... talk about 'it', but—" he looked over his shoulder as if someone was going to magically appear and then at me again "—how do we not? You're here because you couldn't sleep because of ..."

"We just don't. That's how." I fidgeted with the sleeves of my hoodie. "How'd you fall asleep?" I met his eyes.

He held up four fingers. "Four Benadryl."

"That's probably not a good idea."

"I don't think anything about tonight was a good idea, Jorja."

For some reason, that felt like a slap in the face. He was on my side, right? Because I'd die if he wasn't.

I *needed* him on my side. I wanted to scream and argue that it was a great idea—I rid the world of a monster tonight—but I pressed my lips together instead of saying a word.

"Did I say something wrong?" I imagine the look on my face gave me away.

I looked at him and shook my head. I didn't have the energy to overanalyze the details with him. I just wanted to get some rest and fast forward years later when all of this, hopefully, was a case that never got solved, and Jerome Bonovich was forever a missing man.

"I just need sleep, and I wanted to be with you." Those two things were true.

"And what will your mom or people think when you're here the night your father goes missing?"

The corners of my mouth lifted a little. "That I'm a rebellious teenager sneaking out. What girl wouldn't want to be sneaking out with Rush True?" I looked at him through my lashes and was a bit shocked I could still blush with the weight of murder on my chest. I felt a little guilty not telling him the full truth of why I was at his house, but it was better that way. The less he knew, the safer he was. He already held the weight of seeing Jerome kill his mother and not being able to tell. So, what does that say about how I feel about Toby? Don't I want his safety, too? I mean, of course, but I also knew I could count on him to do the hard things. In Rush I found comfort, and with Toby it was dangerous and exciting—something about him felt forbidden. My head started throbbing, causing me to rub my forehead.

Rush kissed my forehead. "Get some rest, Jorja."

"Will you hold me until I fall asleep?" I pleaded in a whisper.

His arms moved around me until I was fully embraced by them. "I'd hold you forever if that's what you wanted."

Melting into him, I had never felt safer. I closed my eyes and allowed his breathing and heartbeat to lull me to sleep.

CHAPTER TWO

Rush

Once Jorja fell asleep, I moved my arm out from under her and slipped out of bed. I needed to go find my brother so we could both be on the same page about what we would tell Dad when he got home. I opened and closed the door quietly and made my way down the hall to his room.

"Toby," I said, lightly knocking on the door. He always kept his door locked. "Tobes," I knocked a few more times.

"What—" I jumped at the sound of his voice beside me. He chuckled. "What are you doing up?"

"If you're out here, why is your door locked?"

He shook his head. "It's not. Did you even try it?" He laughed again.

I turned the knob and sighed. "No, I just assumed. So, what are you doing up?"

"I asked first. I figured you were in there sleeping with your girlfriend."

"She's not my ..." I rubbed my forehead. "We need to figure out what we're gonna tell Dad since she's here."

"That she snuck in."

I nodded. "Right. Duh."

Toby put a hand on my shoulder. "You gotta calm down or you're gonna give us away."

"Give what away?" Dad's voice made us both jump.

Dammit.

I forced a smile. "Heyyy, Dad."

He started taking off the badge from his shirt. "Just spit it out. What are you two heathens up to?"

"Well ..." I started to stammer so Toby jumped in.

"Jorja snuck in my window about two hours ago."

Dad groaned and shook his head. "Of course she did. Where is she right now?" He looked at me.

"Sleeping."

Toby pointed at me. "In his bed. Not mine. See, I'm totally innocent here."

Dad cursed a few times. "I have to take her home. She can't be here. She has enough going on, and being in one of my son's beds and ending up pregnant is the last thing she needs!"

I threw up my hands. "Whoa, do we have to bring up sex? Which we haven't had, might I add."

"Yet. You haven't had sex *yet.* I know how minds your age work. Now, go wake her up."

"Dad—"

"Now!" His voice was so loud, I'm sure it woke her up.

"I'm up. We can go." We all looked toward my bedroom door and saw Jorja standing there with sleepy eyes. She looked at my dad and avoided looking at Toby and me.

Her face was red, making me wonder how long she had been standing there. With my luck, she'd heard the entire conversation. Of course, Toby thought it was hilarious while I stood there with my cheeks full of embarrassment. She'd had a bad enough night—making her uncomfortable or humiliated wasn't my intention.

"I'm sorry," I said quietly as I looked at her.

She shrugged and started nervously fidgeting with the sleeves of her shirt. "It's fine. I shouldn't be here. Officer True is right."

"Finally, someone in the house with some sense," he said, eyeing Toby and me. He looked at Jorja. "I'm sorry, Jorja, but you know I have to bring you home."

"I understand. I just hate ..." Her eyes started to pool with tears as she looked over at Dad. "I just hate being in that house," she said, her voice breaking, and it broke my heart.

"I know, and I wish there were something I could do."

She dabbed her eyes with her sleeves and looked at Toby. When he gave her a slight nod, my chest tightened. What the hell did *that* look mean?

"Alright, boys, back to bed." He looked at us both seriously until we agreed.

Toby went into his room immediately, but I waited in the hall until Dad and Jorja walked out of my sight and I heard the back door open and close.

I went to Toby's door and tried to open it, but it was locked. I beat on the door. "Toby."

"I'm going to bed," he said, loud enough for me to hear.

"Open the door."

It took several seconds before he finally opened it. "What?"

"What the hell was that look?"

He sighed heavily as he leaned against the door frame. "What look, Rush?"

"Jorja. She looked at you and you nodded."

He crossed his arms over his chest. "Are you serious right now?'

I glared at him.

"She looked at me like she needed me to tell her to go, so I nodded. You need to calm the hell down. I know this night has you all jumpy and shit, but you seriously need to just chill. You're gonna give the whole thing away."

"Why are you fully dressed?" I noticed it earlier when I first saw him in the hall but forgot to ask.

"Jorja fell through my window and woke me up. I couldn't go back to sleep so I figured I might as well get dressed."

He was lying. Twin intuition. I looked him over and noticed a fresh burn on his hand. "What's that?" I asked, motioning my hand toward his right one.

He looked at his hand. "I burned it when we burned our clothes earlier."

Still lying. It was too fresh for it to have been from when we burned our stuff.

"We have school tomorrow, Rush. We really need to try to get some sleep. It's five in the morning."

"So, what ... we get like maybe two hours before we have to get up?"

He shrugged as he looked at his hand. "It's better than nothing." Bringing his eyes back to mine, he asked, "Are we done here?"

My brain hurt, and even if I wanted to press him for more answers, it could wait. For now, anyway. "For now."

"I figured as much."

Toby speaking stopped me from starting to walk away.

"Rush, I'm not trying to take Jorja if that's what you're so upset about. We have enough to worry about than to be in a ridiculous fight over a broken girl."

I turned to face him. "Don't talk about her like that."

He scoffed. "Like what? I'm calling her what she is. You can be delusional all you want, but involving her in the middle of some pointless, brotherly feud is the last thing she needs. So, for the sake of everyone's sanity, please drop it. We both know that's what you're really pissed about. This isn't a competition to see who gets the girl. And I need to make it clear that she and I are friends, or at least figuring out how to be friends. I need you to trust me."

I could see the sincerity etched on his face. Toby was right; involving Jorja in our petty rivalry would only bring her unnecessary pain. She deserved better than that, better than being reduced to some prize to be won.

"You're right, it's not about winning or losing her. It's about protecting her."

He nodded slowly, a flicker of compassion in his eyes. "She's been through enough, and there is no telling what's about to happen."

"Maybe trying to get two hours of sleep is a good idea."

He chuckled. "Yeah. School will be interesting."

With that, I headed to my room to try to get some much-needed rest.

CHAPTER THREE

Toby

School was eerily normal. I'm not really sure what I expected it to be like the day after I assisted with murder, but I didn't expect it to feel like any other day. Jorja was her usual force of nature, and her friends followed her around like they worshiped her. She really had no idea the effect she had on people. There weren't many people who could make an entire room stand still and stare the way she could. Some people hated her, some wanted to be her, others loved her. It was sorcery, really.

I drummed my fingers to the music against the steering wheel while I waited on Rush. He had text and said he was checking on Jorja at cheer practice before meeting me. I'd thought about going with him, but that'd be out of character for me, and we all agreed to act normal.

I turned down the radio when I saw my brother walking toward the truck. He tossed his backpack into the back before getting in. He had a bewildered look on his face, and I debated on commenting on it.

"She's fine, before you ask."

That lessened the tension in my bones a little. I put the truck in reverse. "Good."

"It's weirding me out. She acted normal all day long. Everyone did."

I put the truck in drive after backing out of my parking space and started driving. "How exactly did you expect her to act? And her friends always let her set the tone for how they all act. They're all puppets, I swear."

"They're good people, so don't judge them like that, and I know what you're saying, but she never even looked at me in secret like ... You know?"

I looked at him for a moment before averting my eyes back to the road. "Yeah, I get it, but she's right. We just need to go on and let it become something we did but not let it rule our thoughts or actions."

He paused for a moment. "When do you think they'll realize he's missing?" he asked as he stared out the window, lost in thought.

"Her mom will probably figure it out before anyone else. Maybe today. Is he typically home a lot?"

Rush shrugged. "Jorja's never mentioned it."

"Did you see Peter today?"

Rush looked at me and shook his head. "No. With everything that went down, he may never want to show his face at school again."

Memories of the party that night—Brian getting shot, and Jorja finding out it was Peter tormenting her to bring down her family—invaded my mind. How Jorja was handling everything while still being able to be so poised and normal blew me away.

"Any word on how Brian is doing since he was readmitted into the hospital?"

He shook his head. "Nope. It's doubtful anyone will share much information with Jorja since he's being framed for the murder of Mom. It's not fair. I know he didn't do it."

"But you won't say a word."

He nodded but didn't comment.

I drove into town and stopped at a red light, thinking about my brother. Everything going on had to be taking a toll on him while also in the middle of grieving our mother. I grieved for her while she was alive, so I felt no different now. "What about you? Are you okay?" The light turned green, and I forged ahead, waiting for him to answer.

From the corner of my eye, I could see he looked at me. "What do you mean?"

"You're just going through a lot. Why don't we go do something, get our minds off everything with Jorja and Mom's death? We haven't done anything together in a while."

He smiled a little. "What do you want to do?"

"Go camping?"

He laughed. "In the dead of winter?"

Shrugging, I said, "We've done it before. It'll be good to disconnect and hang out."

"What if Jorja needs us?"

"We'll tell her where she can find us if she does."

He sighed and looked out the window. Snow had just started to fall. "Will it look suspicious if people start realizing her dad is missing while we're also camping?"

"Maybe, but investigations would prove we're innocent. Besides, if we are labeled suspects, then it'll keep them off Jorja's back."

"Why'd she do it?" Rush whispered. "Why on earth would she risk everything? If she's caught, her life is over. Not to mention if all the dirty people Jerome was working with find out."

I pulled into our driveway and parked. "Only she knows the answer as to why she did it, but it must've been bad enough for her to follow through with it. The what-ifs are going to drive us insane if we let them. We just need to take it day by day."

"Who knew it'd be as easy as putting a lethal amount of sleeping pills in his drink. It just seems too easy."

And that's when it hit me. As I worked on melting the keys with Dad's welding torch last night, I tried to think of anything Jorja may not have thought of, but I never once thought about the drink. Not until my brother mentioned it.

"Shit."

He looked at me. "What?"

"Do you think she got rid of the drink and the cup?"

He shut his eyes and whispered, "Shit."

"Surely, she did. Right? Did she mention it to you at all?"

He looked at me again. "No. We need to talk to her."

"They have a maid, right?"

Rush nodded.

"You think she already cleaned it up?"

Rush thought for a moment. "Probably, but we should still let Jorja know just in case."

"Did you and her make plans for after practice?"

He shook his head. "She just said she'd text me later."

"Then we'll wait to see if she texts. If she doesn't, we'll find a way to talk to her."

He nodded, but worry still invaded his eyes. "Okay."

"The most important thing right now is that we all remain calm."

He scoffed.

That's where the conversation ended. What else was there to say? It's not like we've done this before. The cup shouldn't be a big deal, unless the maid saw what Jorja did somehow. Or maybe everything would look bad on the maid and she'd become a suspect, which wasn't fair considering she did nothing. Scenarios ran wild through my mind.

Rush put his hand on the handle to open the door just as his phone started ringing. "It's Dad," he said, showing me the screen. He answered it on speaker.

"Where are you two?" He sounded breathless, and the sound of clothes shuffling made it hard to hear him. "*Where are you two?*" he repeated in a shout. I heard a car door open and shut.

"We just pulled up at the house. What's wrong?"

"I just got word that Jerome Bonovich is missing. Where's Jorja?"

"Cheer practice," Rush answered as he kept his eyes on mine.

"Don't say anything to her. We can't issue an official missing person report until it's been at least forty-eight hours. In the meantime, we'll be making every effort to find him. I just wanted you to be aware. Stay home, just in case."

After Rush hung up, we both got out of the truck without a word.

CHAPTER FOUR

Jorja

Against my better judgement, I drove to the hospital after cheer practice. I needed to see Brian, even though I was forbidden to do so. I wasn't even sure if they'd let me see him with the charges he was facing. I knew he didn't kill Rush and Toby's mom, and so did my mother, but Jerome knew enough important people to make sure Brian spent the rest of his life behind bars. I may have killed Jerome, but the damage to Brian had already been done, unless I could prove he was innocent. I'd never let Rush confess he saw Jerome kill his mom, so I had to come up with another idea.

Just as I had expected, getting in to see Brian was damn near impossible. I say *near* because they hadn't met me yet. I'd find a way. I sat in the waiting room, scanning the room and watching the receptionist desk. I watched the way she scanned the room, too. I stood and went to the desk a second time.

"Can someone at least tell me how he is? I have a right to know. I'm his sister."

She looked at me with sympathy, and I didn't like it. I didn't need anyone feeling sorry for me, I needed someone to side with me and let me see him. "I wish I could, but unless you're his legal guardian, I can't. If your mother or father comes, I can share information with them, and they would be able to see him."

They wouldn't be coming here. Maybe once my mother realized Jerome was gone she would, but, until then, I'd have to think of another way. I also had to consider that Brian and I were both being watched. Jerome would never leave us unsupervised when having the goal of framing someone else other than him and we knew the truth. Jerome was no longer a threat if I didn't comply, but the plans he put into motion if I didn't were still very much alive.

I turned to leave and stopped abruptly at the sight of someone that looked familiar walking through the double doors that led to where my brother was. A woman who looked so much like my mother but wasn't. My mind was trailing in so many different directions that it was hard to realize it right away, but when I did, my breath caught in my throat and the heaviness in my chest made it hard to breathe at all.

Olivia.

Dressed in scrubs and moving with a sense of purpose, a figure reminiscent of my long-lost sister walked down the hospital corridor. She kept her head lowered, seemingly preoccupied, her hands fidgeting with the keys in her pocket. But what was she doing here? Olivia had vanished years ago, cutting ties with our family, erasing herself from our lives to escape the suffocating weight of our secrets.

Was it truly her?

It couldn't be.

Yet, the uncanny resemblance, the familiar gestures—undeniable echoes of my sister haunted me.

"Olivia!" I shouted as I tried to keep up with her, but she started running.

A car not paying attention almost hit me, causing me to stop. Tears started to stream down my face as I tried to catch my breath. The car moved past me, and I put my hands on my head as I frantically looked around for Olivia.

She was gone.

By the time I made it to my car and got in, I lost it. The heaviness of everything got the best of me, and I sobbed with my head against the steering wheel. I heard my phone ding several times before I was finally able to calm myself enough to check the notifications. With shaking hands, I unlocked the screen and saw a message from Mom, Toby, and Rush.

Mom: Where are you? You need to come home now. No one has heard from your father, and he's been reported missing by your grandfather.

Toby: I'm sorry I didn't get to talk to you at school today. How are you?

Rush: Call me.

I pulled down the visor and looked at myself in the mirror. I couldn't look like I had been crying when I got home. I decided to only reply to Mom to let her know I was on my way home from a late practice. After composing myself, I started the drive home.

Rush and Toby had to know what was going on because they both sent messages. Toby understood the assignment by messaging me with a general message, but I wanted to smack Rush in the head for sending the message he did. If anyone were watching our phones, which wouldn't surprise me, his would be suspicious. However, people do know he is a cop's son, so if he or Toby mentioned anything about Jerome missing, it'd be expected since we are close, but it was also best to not leave a phone trail about any of it at all.

I turned up the radio, trying to drown out my thoughts about my sister, but it didn't work. What was she doing? Was it really her, or was I just so paranoid about everything my mind made me think it was? The way she kept her head down and ran, though ... Or maybe I was freaking the poor woman out the way I was following her and calling her by name. If it wasn't her, wouldn't they have turned around and told me I was mistaken? If I didn't end up behind bars, I knew I'd be a prisoner to my thoughts forever.

When I pulled into the driveway, I noticed it was lined with cop cars, Officer True's being one of them. I grabbed my cheer bag from the back seat and coached myself the entire way inside, reminding myself to act surprised.

As soon as I entered, I was engulfed in my mother's arms as she cried. "Oh, Jorja, I'm so glad you're home!"

I dropped the cheer bag to the floor and wrapped my arms around her, hiding my face against her shoulder, relishing in the brief moment I wouldn't have to put on an act. We pulled away, and Officer True, along with two other officers, came into the foyer.

"We're done with the walk-through and there are no signs of him or foul play here. We'll forward the information to the FBI since they are involved now," Officer True's voice had taken on a disgruntled tone with the mention of the FBI, "and I'm sure they'll be contacting you within the next day or two. Just know if you don't hear anything right away, don't panic, we're all actively searching and contacting the authorities," he said, while looking at my mother—he never looked at me—and then they left.

I didn't know what to make of Officer True not looking or saying anything to me at all. Did he know? Did the guys tell him? And why was the FBI involved in a local case like this? I looked at Mom as she started to cry some more.

She wrapped her arms around herself. "Jorja, this isn't good. This is going to get ugly. Someone must've tipped off more than just the local authorities."

"Maybe he's on a job somewhere and lost service," I suggested, as I picked up the cheer bag I had dropped.

She shook her head. "His car is at the funeral home."

"Maybe he rode with someone else. You know the super-secret jobs he goes on."

Her eyes were gravely serious. "Jorja, *no one* has heard from him."

The reality of what that meant weighed heavily on my chest. The cartel, all of his contacts he's in cohorts with every single day, none of them had heard from him. I didn't consider how quickly his disappearance would catch fire. The revelation that I didn't consider much at all stung. I needed my brother and his advice. I needed to figure out if that was Olivia and why she was in the same hospital as Brian. I could feel my sanity crumbling and needed to get away from my mother.

"Are we safe?" I asked quietly.

"We're never safe." She shivered. "I need to make some phone calls. It may be best for you to not stay here and go stay with your grandparents."

Panic set in. I'd die before I go stay with them. "I'll be fine. I—"

"It's not your decision to make." Her voice was low and stern, and I knew I wouldn't win the argument. "Go pack a bag, and I'll let you know if you'll drive there or if they'll send a driver for you."

"Mom, please," I begged, despite knowing it wouldn't help.

"My job is to protect you, and with everything that happened before his disappearance, I don't know how safe any of us are. He could be up to anything, and one place I know you'll be safe is at your grandparents."

"Yeah right, because they're more insane than Jerome!" Not to mention that they aren't really my grandparents after all. They never were. "Do they even know that I'm not really their granddaughter?"

"No, and you will not tell them. Now, go upstairs, get packed, and wait for my direction."

"And what about you? What about Brian? You know he was innocent, and—"

Her lips quivered, and her body began to tremble harder. "Do not question me! Everything I do, I do it because it's strategic and right. Now go!"

Without another word, I headed to my room to pack. Arguing would serve no purpose.

32

CHAPTER FIVE

Rush

I stood from the couch as soon as Dad walked in. It was past midnight, but Toby and I couldn't sleep so we watched movies to try to pass the time. Toby stayed seated, looking up at Dad. He took off his badge and set it on the end table before sitting in the recliner and putting his head in his hands. My brother and I exchanged a brief look of concern before looking at him again.

I sat again. "Dad?"

"You boys should be asleep," he said, finally looking at us. Hours of stress were evident in the bags under his eyes.

"Is Jorja okay?" Toby asked.

"You haven't heard from her? I figured by now she would have contacted one of you."

Toby and I both shook our heads.

He nodded and sighed heavily. "She has a lot going on."

"But she's okay?" Toby asked again.

Dad looked at him. "She was in shock and worried, but she was fine. I'll be pulling a lot of extra hours for the foreseeable future. We're starting a search in the morning, and now the FBI is involved. Someone contacted them, but we all know they're only involved because of the connections the Bonovich family has with them. They have connections everywhere. I can't even trust the guys on my squad."

I didn't know what to say. Two people in the room knew exactly where the body was. No matter how angry I was with Jorja for doing this and risking so much, the fact that she murdered the man who took my mother from me, not to mention the countless other people he killed, she did the world a favor, and I could never repay her.

"I suggest you boys try and rest. You're going to school tomorrow regardless of everything going on." He stood and stretched. "I'm going to try to sleep while I can."

Toby and I watched as he started to leave the room but stopped just before entering the hallway to look over his shoulder at us. "There will be no sneaking out or any funny business from either of you. Got it?"

"Yes, sir," we both said.

He gave us his best "I'll kick your asses" look before rounding the corner and leaving us alone. I looked up at Toby when he stood.

He yawned before talking. "I'm gonna try to get some sleep. If you hear from her, will you let me know?"

I took my phone off the armrest of the couch and looked at it, hoping to see a message from Jorja. "Yeah ... same to you."

He nodded and left the living room. I stared at the message that was delivered. It never took her long to message me back. Dad said she was fine, but he didn't know our secret. There was no way she was okay. She had to be losing her mind being in that house and wondering what would happen next. I sent another text, despite telling myself not to.

Me: Jorja, please call me. I'm worried about you.

My heart sped up when a message came in almost immediately.

Jorja: I'm ok, Rush. Just in shock... I'm so tired but can't sleep.
Me: I wish I could fix this.
Jorja: Of course you do. You know, you can't save me from everything, right?
Me: I'd die trying.
Jorja: Same.

Me: What do you mean?

Jorja: That I'd save you from everything, too, if I could... and even if I couldn't, I'd die trying.

That was the first time Jorja had ever said something that intimate to me, and even in the midst of the hell we created, it made me smile and hold out hope for us. That if anyone could work, it'd be her and me. No obstacle could ever stop us because we'd always have each other even in the most vulnerable and scariest moments. I wondered how long this moment would last with her because she'd most likely talk herself out of it in a second.

Me: **We should both get some sleep.**

Jorja: **Yeah, we should.**

Me: **I didn't wake you up, did I?**

Jorja: **No, I was awake. I'm sorry I didn't respond earlier. I had to pack and make sure I had the phone hidden. I just laid down and was able to sneak it back out.**

The secret phone Toby and I got her before all of this happened was still coming in handy.

Me: **Pack?**

Jorja: **I can't say where I am.**

Me: **Will you be at school tomorrow?**

Jorja: **Yes.**

Me: Are you at home?

Jorja: I can't text personal information right now, just in case. Let's get some sleep. Don't worry, I'm safe.

Me: We should both get some sleep.

Jorja: Rush?

Me: Yeah?

Jorja: Thank you for everything.

I scrolled back to the message where she said she'd save me from everything. My eyes lingered there for several beautiful moments. I smiled because I knew she meant it or she wouldn't have said it.

Me: Goodnight, Jorja.

Jorja: Night.

CHAPTER SIX

Toby

As I walked through the hall to my next class, I heard my name, but before I could see who said it, I was being pulled into the janitor's closet. The door shut, and it was pitch black. I didn't have to hear a voice or see her face to know it was Jorja. Her presence alone was unlike anything else in the entire world. Plus, she smelled like roses and vanilla—how I imagined heaven to smell. I cringed at the sappy tone of my thoughts and swore I'd never use that pickup line out loud.

"I've seen this movie scene before," I said through laughter.

She clasped her hand over my mouth. "Shhh!"

I licked the palm of her hand, making her shriek before she started laughing. "Toby!"

"Aren't we supposed to be whispering?"

She playfully shoved my chest. "I can't believe you did that."

I took my phone from my back pocket and turned on the flashlight, putting it under my chin to dramatically illuminate my face. "Are we gonna talk about ... murder?" I asked in the creepiest, lowest voice I could muster.

She rolled her beautiful eyes and took the phone from me. "Be serious."

I put on a serious face. "Yes, ma'am."

"I couldn't text or talk to you in front of anyone, but I need to talk to someone to work all of this out in my head."

"What's going on?"

She tucked some hair behind her ear and handed my phone back to me. "I think I saw my sister yesterday."

My eyebrows shot up. "Olivia?"

She looked at me oddly. "Yeah, how'd you know her name?"

"Jorja, everyone knows her name. Olivia Bonovich is famous for disappearing from Grove Hills."

"I didn't even think about that. Now Jerome is missing ... The law is going to be all over this."

"Where'd you see her?"

"The hospital. I was trying to see Brian, but they wouldn't let me. I need to talk to him."

"Does Rush know about any of this?"

She shook her head and looked at the door when the noise from the hall started to die down. The tardy bell was about to ring. "We need to get to class. Can we meet later to talk about it?"

I wanted to ask why she was talking to me and not Rush, but, instead, I agreed. "Where and when?"

"I have cheer practice, but I'll skip it. I have to be back at my grandparents' as soon as cheer practice is over, so let's meet after school. I just don't want Rush involved in any of it."

"Why?"

"Because the less that he knows the better, and I don't need him finding any more reasons to go to the cops and tell them he saw Jerome kill your mother."

"Okay, but we ride home together."

"Take him home and find an excuse to go to town. Meet me at the spot me and my friends hang out at the lake at four o'clock."

"And what if your friends show up there?"

She shook her head. "They won't. Not on a weeknight."

I rubbed the back of my neck. "Alright ... I'll be there at four." Remembering the cup, I quickly said, "Before you go, the cup you poisoned Jerome with, did you get rid of it?"

She nodded. "When I got back to my house, I shattered it and flushed the pieces down the toilet."

"Is that a good idea?"

She laughed. "It doesn't matter now. It's done." She hugged me quickly. "Now go out first and text me to let me know the hall is clear, but just say 'how are you' or something not suspicious in the text. I don't need anyone seeing us come out of the closet together."

I adjusted the backpack strap on my right shoulder and went out into the hall. No one ever paid attention to me, so I didn't cause a single head to turn.

Once I rounded the corner, I text her.

Me: You ok?

I was sure she had already made it into the hall, but of course I had to question if anyone saw us go in and out. The rumors would spread like wildfire before the end of the day if they did. Rush would completely lose his mind, and part of me hated keeping any of it from him. If I told him, there was no way he wouldn't try to get involved, and I didn't want Jorja to lose her trust in me. She could count on me, and I wouldn't risk her thinking otherwise or my brother risking his safety.

I checked my phone: **4:05**. Leaning my back against the passenger door of my truck, I looked to my left when I heard tires on gravel. I smiled softly when I saw her car. Meeting her alone made my heart speed up in ways it probably shouldn't. Even if she hadn't admitted it to herself yet, she cared more for my brother than she ever could me. Sometimes when I couldn't sleep at night, I'd think about how everything could be different. I wished I could go back in time and instead of pushing her away because she was popular and rich, allowed her to get to know me better.

I pushed off the truck as she parked, walked over to her car, and, once she killed the engine, opened the door for her. She smiled up at me before getting out. I shut the door behind her, and she motioned for me to follow her. Once we were well into the thicket of tall pines, she stopped walking and turned to face me.

"What is it?" she asked as she looked at me. "Your eyes are all scrunchy."

I chuckled and shook my head. "I don't know why ... Oh, yeah, maybe because we're sneaking behind my brother's back, constantly figuring out ways to keep the murder covered up, meeting in the woods ..." I put my hands into my pockets where I could remind them that pulling her into a hug or holding her hand would be wrong.

"This is a mess."

"Ya think?"

She looked up at me, tears pooling in her eyes. "I'm sorry I keep involving you. I can figure it out on my own. This shouldn't be a burden we share."

"But it is, Jorja. I can't just pretend nothing happened. We're in this together now."

And I loved it and hated it at the same time. What kind of man did that make me? What did it say about how I felt about her? No matter how dark this all was, I did it because I cared about her and out of vengeance for my mother. I know without a doubt she'd do it for me, and the reasoning behind my actions was right, even if the law would disagree.

"Thank you."

I smiled softly. "You're welcome. Now let's talk about why we're here."

"I don't know what to do. I need to see my brother, and I thought I could figure out a way to see him, but I'm at a loss. They said only my parents can get information on him, but my mom is beside herself, and she's shipped me off to my grandparents. Toby ... what do you know about my family?"

I shrugged. I could admit to some of the things my dad had told me, but all of that was confidential. Jorja would have to be the one to tell me because I'd never break that trust with Dad. "Just enough to know they're criminals with no consequences."

"I'm going to tell you everything, but I need our phones off."

I nodded and turned off my phone and watched her turn hers off, too.

"They run a drug cartel. The funeral home brings in a decent living because my grandparents own three more in surrounding towns, but the one in Grove is used as a front for a drug smuggling operation. That's where all our money comes from. It's a family affair, running several generations deep. They hide drugs in freshly dug graves as a way to transport. Coordinates are given which lead those that pick up to where they are. There are so many drugs hidden in coffins in storage. Once you're in this business, the only way out is to die. I could never leave here because I know too much. It's like every single Bonovich is trapped in this unyielding cyclone of chaos; this relentless merry-go-round of torment with no escape." Tears started to fall down her cheeks, and my hands forgot the rules I set a moment ago. I wiped her tears away and wrapped her in my arms.

"Why are you being so nice to me?" she asked as her hands clung to the back of my shirt. She kept her face buried against my chest. "I've asked you for so much and don't deserve your loyalty."

"If you didn't deserve it, I wouldn't be here. I need you to stop this self-destruction thing you do with me. We've had our differences, but it's in the past. Plus, why wouldn't I want to help aid in the murder of the man who killed my mother?"

She pulled back just enough to look up at me. "How are you doing with that?"

"I'm sad for my brother. Seeing him grieve makes me grieve. I don't hurt for her, though. She was never a mother to me." I hated talking about her, so I quickly changed the subject. "Let's talk about why you asked me to come here."

Jorja nodded and stepped back, causing my arms to fall back to my sides. "I have to find a way to make sure the police know Brian is innocent, but, first, I need to talk to him. I also need to find out if that was really Olivia. Her hair was shorter and darker than I remember it, but I just know it was her."

"Let's—" I stopped talking when we heard tires on gravel coming our way.

CHAPTER SEVEN

Jorja

I kept my eyes on Toby's. I didn't think any of my friends would be at the lake during the week—they never were. Plus, the girls were at cheer practice. I jumped a little when I heard a car door shut. Toby put his finger to his lips and protectively moved me behind him. *Please don't be Rush. Please don't be Rush. Please don't be—*

"Jorja? Rush? Toby?" I heard Tommy's voice echo through the air.

"Shit," Toby mumbled and rubbed his forehead. "This looks bad."

"We'll explain." I stepped out from behind him.

"Explain what exactly?"

He was right. We couldn't tell him anything. When I didn't respond, he motioned for me to follow him.

"Just let me talk. I'll figure something out."

I followed him out of the woods, and when we came into Tommy's view, he crossed his arms over his chest. "What do we have here?"

"I asked Jorja to meet me here to talk," Toby said calmly.

Tommy looked at me. "Are you okay?"

I nodded. "Yeah."

"Don't you have practice?" Tommy asked me.

"I skipped it to talk to Toby."

"Where's Rush?"

"At home," Toby admitted.

"So, this is exactly what it looks like, huh?"

I hated the disappointment in Tommy's eyes. Rush and he were basically best friends now, and I know he's always been rooting for Rush and me, but he needed to let that go. Not that I was denying I had feelings for Rush, but because he had no idea what I was dealing with which was way bigger than who I was or wasn't dating.

"No, it's not what it looks like," I said, growing more frustrated by the second. Why couldn't I just be talking to a friend? Why did it have to look like something? "Toby is one of my friends, and he needed to talk to me. Rush doesn't have to be here to have a conversation with his brother."

"So, Rush knows you both are here alone?" Tommy turned his attention to Toby.

"No, he doesn't, and I'd appreciate it if it stayed that way. I'm worried about my brother, and I needed to talk to Jorja because Rush won't listen to me. He's been suppressing his emotions about the death of our mother and the things he saw when she was killed. I think he needs help. He can't sleep unless he downs a handful of pills. I know Jorja can talk some sense into him."

Tommy cursed. "I didn't know he was having such a hard time."

Toby shrugged. "I know you didn't. He won't talk about it, and he isn't the type of guy to project his issues on others."

I knew Toby was covering for me, but what he was saying didn't sound like a lie. A wave of sadness seeped into my bones. It felt as though an invisible hand had gripped my heart tightly, squeezing it until it threatened to burst through my chest. It gave me even more reason to keep Rush out of this mess as much as possible.

Tommy's eyes softened. "Sorry I assumed otherwise."

"Why are you here anyway?" I asked, still worried about Rush. I knew what Toby said had to be true because when I snuck into their house the other night, Rush had a huge bottle of Benadryl on his nightstand and said he took some to sleep. I didn't think much of it because of what happened that night, but if he was doing it every night and taking more than he should since his mother's death, that wasn't good.

Tommy shrugged and kicked a few loose rocks around. "Just coming here to avoid going home. Dad's drinking has gotten worse which results in all these questions about college, his disappointment in me, and how I need to be a man and shit. I just needed some silence before going home. But enough about that, how are you? Any word on Jerome or your brother since we talked at lunch?"

"No." I wrapped my arms around myself. "I should probably head to my grandparents'. They made it very clear that I have to be there on time after practice."

Toby looked at me with worry-filled eyes. "I'll walk you to the car."

I nodded and looked at Tommy. "I'll talk to Rush and figure out what's going on, but please keep seeing us here to yourself. I don't want him mad at Toby for telling me."

"Lips are sealed." Tommy faked zipping his lips.

I hugged him goodbye and watched him drive away before walking with Toby to my car.

When we got to my car, Toby opened the door and rested his arm on the top of the window as I got in. "We didn't finish the conversation," he said as he looked down at me.

I cranked the engine and looked up at him. "We'll have to finish it later. Was that true what you said about Rush?"

He looked at the ground and sighed heavily before looking at me again. "Yeah."

"I'll talk to him." I looked at the steering wheel. "If you have any ideas about getting me in to see Brian, let me know."

"I will. Be careful heading to your grandparents'. How long do you have to stay there, anyway?"

I shrugged and looked at him again. "Who knows."

"Text me when you make it there."

I nodded and watched as he shut the door.

After making it past the gate and driving down the three-mile driveway, I pulled up to my grandparents' estate. I parked my car in the garage, next to my grandfather's black Denali.

I got my bags from the backseat and headed inside to find my grandmother sitting near the fireplace in the common room sipping on a glass of brandy. She looked away from the fire and her blue eyes found me.

"Dinner will be ready soon, sweetheart." She lowered the glass to her leg, her hand trembling, causing the ice to rattle. She was getting so much older, but the effects of age were becoming more obvious no matter how much she paid to try to hide it.

The last thing I wanted to do was sit at a dinner table with my grandfather and her, but I wouldn't have a choice. I wondered what they'd do if I told them I sunk their precious son into the bottom of the river. If I had known a way to hell, I would've hand delivered him to the devil himself. "Yes, ma'am."

"There's still no word on your father. Your grandfather has been in his office on the phone all day. How are you holding up?"

My mother made it very clear that they weren't aware that I knew he wasn't really my father, and I was to act heartbroken instead of relieved. "Just trying to keep my mind off it. It's hard."

Tears trickled down her cheeks. "Go get yourself cleaned up and presentable for dinner." She quickly wiped her eyes and brought her cup to her lips. I went and kissed her cheek, a requirement of hers since Olivia, Brian, and I were toddlers.

As soon as I got to the guest room that would be mine for the foreseeable future, I set my bags down and text Toby.

Me: **I made it to my grandparents.**

While I waited to hear back, I started getting ready. My grandparents expected you to attend dinner dressed as if you were about to walk down the red carpet. It was ridiculous, but the more I became aware of how corrupt this life was, the more I realized this is what people who think they're important with too much damn money did. Anything to feel superior and find a thrill in something. It was disgusting.

I looked at myself in the mirror after slipping on a fitted, black, satin dress and combed my fingers through my loose curls. My makeup was still on, and I hoped my grandmother didn't notice I didn't touch it up. After putting on some red lipstick to throw her off, I sat on the edge of the bed to put on my heels. I was just about to walk out of the room when I heard my phone buzz from the dresser.

Becca: Are you ok? This is crazy! It's all over the news. My parents are flipping out. There are cops at your house... It's a good thing you're not home!

I didn't have time to text back. If I didn't arrive at dinner promptly at seven o'clock, I'd have to hear an entire lecture about being on time.

When I came into the dimly lit dining room, I found my grandparents seated at the candle-lit table. My grandfather sat at the head of the table in a large chair that greatly favored a throne with red velvet fabric and intricate carvings. My grandmother sat on the opposite end of the long, rectangular table in a chair like his, just a tad smaller. Each side was lined with seven, dark mahogany chairs that matched the table. I sat on the right side in the middle. It was odd having dinner with them alone. Usually, the table was full of family or important people at their dinner parties. To my left was where Brian would sit and to my right was Olivia's chair she'd been absent from for several years. Mom and Jerome would sit across from us. The silence in the room somehow became deafening, and the ache in my chest for my brother grew stronger. *Stay strong.*

I forced a smile in my grandfather's direction. "Good evening, Grandfather."

"Jorja, you look magnificent tonight. You look more like your mother every time I see you. Speaking of your mother, how is she holding up?"

I took the fabric napkin and unfolded it, placing it onto my lap. "As well as you'd expect. How are you?"

"I'm exhausted. I've made every attempt to find out where he is, but no one has seen him. I'm beginning to believe it was nothing short of foul play. Someone—"

"Don't speak that way," Grandmother scolded him. "We are holding out every ounce of hope that our son will be returned without a scratch. There are many possible scenarios. We are checking the tunnels."

I raised both brows in her direction. "Tunnels?"

She cleared her throat and took a drink of her wine. "Nothing, dear."

Grandfather gave her a look that said they'd be having words later.

The maid walked in with a cart holding our plates. She didn't make eye contact with a soul in the room, only put our plates before us. I wanted to tell her I felt her pain, that if I were her, I'd run as far away from this family as I could. We'd been through a lot of maids at our house, and I often wondered what happened to them when they left. I never saw them again, and Grove was small. I remembered hearing Jerome talk to my mother about a maid once and making the comment that she knew too much. I swallowed hard at the realization of what probably happened to them.

"Jorja, we need to discuss an issue that has arisen," Grandfather said, before taking a long drink of his whiskey.

"About?" I took a bite of my food and waited.

"After speaking with the school—"

"Why would you speak to my school?"

"Young ladies don't speak out of turn, especially when a man is speaking to them," he scolded.

My blood started to boil, but I remained calm.

"After speaking to your school," he continued, "I found out some troubling news. Is there a reason you are fond of the True boys?"

"They're my friends."

The look of disapproval on his face made my heartbeat faster. "With the unfortunate events of their mother's death and now the disappearance of your father—"

I knew where this was going. I didn't care if I broke his stupid rule. "You can't forbid me to see them."

"If you keep speaking out of turn and using a tone such as that, there will be consequences. I can, and I—"

"You won't!" I didn't give myself time to think about what he meant by that; I spoke too quickly. As my grandfather stood from his chair and came to where I was, my grandmother never stopped eating, acting as if everything was completely normal and okay.

I looked up at him, ready to challenge whatever it was he was about to say, but, instead, he slapped me across my face. I yelped and held my hand over the part of my skin that stung.

I will not cry.

I will not cry.

I will not cry.

I never took my eyes off his cold ones.

He walked back over to his chair, adjusted his suit jacket, and sat back down.

"Now, as I was saying, you are to stop seeing those boys. Too many conflicting interests with that family, and no granddaughter of mine will be seen with scrapers like them."

"Scrapers?" I asked, still fighting back tears. I wanted to argue. I wanted to tell him he had no right, but I remained silent.

"Poor people. We are a distinguished family, and we will not tarnish our name with the likes of them. If I find out you're still hanging out with them, I will handle it, and you won't like it. I will also pull you from public school and put you in a private school upstate."

I looked at my grandmother who continued to eat. Did the women in the family not fight back?

I almost made it known that I knew Jerome wasn't my father, that I wasn't legitimately a part of this disgusting family, but now wasn't a good time. It was better to be quiet and devise a plan. They spoke about tunnels which only told me there were more secrets to this family than I originally thought.

"Do you understand, Jorja, or shall I remind you once more who is boss here? We are doing all of this to protect you and the family. Understood?"

It was right then and there that I vowed to myself to take this family down. I wouldn't run like Olivia or obey like the rest of the women. I moved my hand from my cheek and could still feel the heat radiating from it. I sat tall, lifting my chin slightly in his direction. "Understood."

The rest of dinner was quiet, which was for the best. It allowed my mind to play with all of the ways I could burn this kingdom down.

THIS LITTLE SECRET

CHAPTER EIGHT

Rush

I got off the tailgate when I saw a black limo pulling in front of the school. In my gut, I knew exactly who it was, but why wasn't she driving her car? Toby continued to lean against the front of the truck as he watched. I went and stood next to him.

Normally, Jorja and I would walk to class, but when she exited the car, she was escorted by the driver inside the school. "What the hell," I muttered.

"Rush," I heard Tommy and turned around to face him and the rest of the group walking over. "What was that all about?"

I looked at Becca. She'd have more information than any of us. "Do you know?"

She shook her head. "She never mentioned anything about being driven to school."

Everyone looked at Toby, and he shrugged. "Rush would know more than me."

I shook my head. "Not a clue."

Without another word, Toby walked off and headed toward the school.

Wren watched him then looked at me. "Why does he hate us so much?"

"He doesn't hate anyone; he just prefers to stay to himself."

Jena used her phone camera to fix her lip gloss then looked at Wren. "I'm going to work my magic and convert him."

I chuckled. "You're going to convert my brother? To what exactly?"

Jena screwed the lid of her lip gloss back on and put it into her hot pink purse. "To hang out with us. Jorja thinks the world of him, so he must be a good person."

Becca burst into laughter. "That's only part of the truth! You've been saying for weeks how you wanted to—"

Jena covered Becca's mouth with her hand before she could say more. "Becca! Shhh! Not in front of his brother!"

I laughed but didn't comment. If I had a dollar for every time someone said they wanted to get with my brother, I'd be rich. We were identical twins, but something about the mystery of him made the girls go crazy.

Tommy looked at all of us. "Let's get to class, and Rush and I can talk to her when we get to first period."

Beck took Becca's hand in his, indicating they were back together, but their relationship status seemed as changeable as the wind.

We all headed into the building, completely silent. I missed Jorja being beside me, making everyone laugh. The group was tight, but without her there, we were unbalanced.

I felt like I couldn't make it to the classroom fast enough, only to be disappointed when I didn't see Jorja there. I looked at Tommy as we took our normal seats toward the back. He shrugged and sat down. Jorja's seat in the middle of us remained empty even after the tardy bell rang.

I couldn't focus on a thing the teacher was saying. I jumped when Tommy threw a pencil at me, causing the entire class to start laughing. The teacher said my name, and that's when it registered she had been taking attendance.

"Here," I got out quickly and laughed it off, trying my hardest to play it cool.

The secretary's voice over the intercom caused the room to go silent.

"Mrs. Crosby, please don't mark Jorja Bonovich absent. She is in the office getting her schedule changed."

"Okay, thank you," Mrs. Crosby answered and then stood from her desk to start class.

My heart fell to my feet.

Why?

Why on earth did her schedule have to be changed?

I looked at Tommy as he moved his things to where Jorja normally sat so we were sitting side-by-side. "Something isn't right," he said quietly as he sat down in his seat.

"We'll find a way to talk to her later." At least, I hoped we would.

I didn't see Jorja the rest of the day. I heard rumors that she left for lunch and then came back for the rest of her classes. Becca said she saw her in the hall, but when she tried to talk to her, Jorja told her that she'd have to wait until practice. Jorja didn't respond to any of my texts, or anyone else's, according to the group. Toby headed home, and I asked to catch a ride with Tommy so we could wait up and try to see Jorja after practice.

I looked at the time on the radio and got out of the car to wait for her to walk out of the building. Tommy came and stood next to me. The same limo came pulling in and parked in front of the gym.

I started to walk, but Tommy grabbed my arm, stopping me. "Where'ya goin? I think it's obvious she can't talk." He let go of my arm.

"I'm about to figure out what the hell is going on."

I saw Jorja walk out and watched her talking to Becca. When she made eye contact with me, her smile faded. She quickly looked at the driver who was opening the door for her, and then at me again. We both stood there, frozen, staring at one another until the driver got her attention and motioned for her to get into the car.

And then she was gone.

Becca waited until the car pulled away and came over to us.

"Hey," she said as she adjusted the strap of the bag on her shoulder. "Before you ask, it's complicated."

"Just tell me what's going on," I pleaded.

"Jorja has been forbidden to speak to you or Toby."

My jaw tensed. "What?"

"I'm so sorry, Rush. Jorja told me to tell you and Toby that she'd find a way to see you, but, until then, do not attempt to contact her."

"But she has a secret phone."

She shook her head. "Not anymore. Her grandparents found it."

"Is she okay?" Tommy asked.

Becca's eyes turned cold. "I don't think so. She was so distant, like her head was somewhere else during practice. Yesterday, she seemed normal.

Today, it was as if she were a person I had never met before."

This was getting out of hand. I wished I could tell them everything. We needed all the help we could get. The more on our side, the better.

I looked at Tommy when he started to talk. "We need to have a meeting. I'm texting the group and letting everyone know to meet at the lake at eight o'clock."

Becca looked so worried. "I think that's a great idea. Something is majorly wrong."

"Should I invite my brother?" I asked.

"Yes," Tommy said as he stared at his phone and started texting.

Becca and I both looked at our phones when they dinged.

Tommy to the group: The lake at 8:00.

CHAPTER NINE

Toby

When I pulled up at the lake, I parked next to Tommy's car. My old Chevy looked out of place in the line of expensive cars. Everyone was already waiting by the fire, and as I got closer, Rush came over to walk the rest of the way with me.

"What's this all about?" I asked him.

"Helping Jorja," he said as we got to the group.

"No shit. Specifically?"

Jena smiled and waved at me. "Hey, Tobias."

"Hello." I looked at all the others, making sure not to look at her too long. She made me uncomfortable.

Tommy stood from the log he was sitting on and looked at me. "Before we start talking, I need to make sure you understand how our group works. What is said at the lake stays at the lake."

"And what happens if I tell all of my friends?" I said it with a slight smile, but none of them understood I was joking. I cleared my throat. "It was a joke."

Beck eyed me suspiciously. "I don't know, guys, are you sure we can trust him?"

Becca nudged Beck gently. "Jorja trusts him, babe. Of course we can."

Rush nodded in agreement. "You can all trust my brother."

Wren sat down on a log and looked up at me, studying me. "You're a part of the group now, you realize that right, Twin?"

"Why do I feel like I'm not being given a choice?"

Jena giggled. "You catch on quick."

Tommy pulled a flask from the pocket inside of his jacket and took a quick drink. "We all know what happened with Jorja and the Ellisons. Then her brother was shot at the party and is now being framed for the death of Rush and Toby's mother. We know it wasn't him, Rush has made it very clear that he saw Jerome Bonovich kill her, but he promised Jorja and his dad he wouldn't go to the police about it because then he would be a target."

I listened, careful not to say anything because I didn't know what all they knew.

Tommy continued, "Jerome is missing, Jorja is being forced to live with her grandparents, and now she is being driven everywhere and not allowed to talk to Rush or Toby. Jorja was normal yesterday, but today she wasn't herself at all. Something big is going on, and we're going to figure it out. She would do this for any of us here. If anyone knows anything I haven't mentioned, please tell me. All the information we have the better so we can figure out what's going on."

I didn't look at Rush. I couldn't give any indication of knowing where Jerome was.

Becca spoke first. "All I know, since I live the closest to her, is that her house has been swarmed with police and investigators and she told me to tell Rush and Toby that she can't talk to them, and her grandparents found her phone."

"They did?" I looked at Rush.

He looked down at the ground. "I didn't want to tell you on the phone."

"Why would they want to keep her from us?"

"The only thing that makes sense," Tommy said, "is that your mother was killed by her father, and with him missing, it looks suspicious."

I didn't like how everyone was staring at me, waiting to see how I'd handle the news. I didn't like allowing my emotions to be on display like this but keeping Jorja away from me and my brother changed everything, and I wasn't sure how long I'd be able to keep a poker face on.

"Does anyone know where her grandparents live?" I asked.

"Toby, we can't go there," Rush said harshly. "You know we can't."

"Where do they live?" I asked again.

"I've been there before, but the security is unlike anything I've ever seen," Becca said, keeping her eyes on mine. "Rush is right. You can't go there. None of us can. You have to be invited."

Nothing was impossible. I knew exactly who I needed to talk to.

"Brian." All eyes were on me now. "We need to find a way to talk to him."

Jorja was adamant that she speak to him. I wanted to tell them all about the conversation we had and never finished, but I didn't know if she wanted them to know about the possibility of her sister being back, so I kept that part to myself.

Tommy took another drink from his flask. Rush mentioned his dad was an alcoholic, and it seemed as though Tommy would be following in his footsteps. Everyone stared at the fire before Beck broke the silence by asking Tommy to pass the flask around. When it got to me, I passed it without indulging. I watched my brother take a long drink and frowned. I knew this was stressful, but we needed clear heads not muddied by liquor.

Tommy started to speak as he put the flask back inside his jacket pocket. "Every day we will meet here, same time. Tonight, I want everyone thinking about a way to get to Brian. Tomorrow, we'll devise a plan."

I started laughing. I couldn't help it. "When do we get a Mystery Machine van like on Scooby-Doo?"

It took everyone a second to understand what I meant before they all started laughing.

"Twin is funny," Wren said, continuing to laugh.

"And sexy," Jena said with a wink.

Tommy chuckled, shaking his head. "You'll get used to her. I promise. She's—"

"I've never heard you complain," Jena said, causing Tommy to blush.

"Anyway ..." Tommy said, his cheeks still red. "Tomorrow. Eight o'clock," he said, eyeing all of us.

We all agreed.

CHAPTER TEN

Jorja

I sat at the vanity and brushed my wet hair, looking at myself in the mirror. I barely recognized myself—my mind becoming a deadly disease. As soon as I felt fear creeping in, I closed my eyes, took a few calming breaths, and reminded myself of the plan. I'd play nice and comply with the rules set in place. *For now.* It was all a part of my plan to take them down. Even if it took me years, I'd uncover every secret capable of burying them under the weight of hidden truths.

I'd end them.

I looked over my shoulder when there was a knock on the door. "Jorja, can I come in?"

I stood quickly when I heard Mom's voice. "Yes?" I said, more eagerly than I had intended. I should be angry with her, but seeing someone that shared my blood was something I didn't realize I needed so badly at that moment.

As soon as she entered, I flung myself into her arms and hugged her tightly.

"Are you okay?" she asked against the side of my head.

"Yes," I lied. I was far from okay. "I've missed you."

She pulled back enough to cup my face in her hands, keeping her voice low. "I'm sorry I sent you away like that. I panicked. Our house is an entire crime scene. They had the dogs there today smelling his belongings to begin the search. I don't know how long you'll have to stay here, but it's still the safest option." She let her hands fall to her side as we separated.

"I understand. It's fine," I said, matching her low tone. It wasn't fine, but being here would be the best way to find all the skeletons they were hiding. "But what about you? Shouldn't you stay here, too?"

"I'm going to be back and forth. I need to be home to cooperate with the FBI and search efforts."

I wrapped my arms around myself and nodded. "They won't let me see Rush or Toby."

She didn't look surprised. "I agree with that decision. Too many conflicting interests."

I didn't respond. Arguing would get me nowhere.

"You didn't tell them you know Jerome isn't your father, did you?"

I shook my head.

"Thank you for keeping that to yourself. I'm so scared, Jorja. He was so angry that night ... He could be anywhere. Up to anything."

He wasn't. She was safe from him now.

"It's going to be okay, Mom."

She smiled a little. "Part of me hopes he's dead. Gone forever." She covered her mouth and gasped. "I shouldn't have said that." I hated how her hands trembled.

Telling her what I had done was on the tip of my tongue.

I almost said it.

Almost.

"Do you have contact with anyone he had contact with?" I hoped she knew what I meant. I didn't really know how to explain it any other way.

"No. Only the men in the family deal with that."

I wondered what her parents thought of all this. "What about Gran and Gramps? Have you told them what's going on?"

She shrugged. "They know he's missing."

"What'd they say?"

She laughed coldly. "I told you so."

My eyes widened. "I didn't think they knew about anything other than the funeral home business?"

She shook her head. "They don't, but they've never liked your fath—Jerome. They aren't stupid. They may not know details, but they have always known something wasn't right. When I dated Jerome, they did everything they could to keep me from staying with him. Love is such a stupid thing."

I hadn't seen her parents in years. The most contact we had were cards for our birthdays and major holidays. They distanced themselves from us, but now I understood why. This family was destructive.

"Was Jerome always such a villain?"

Her smile was sad. "Knowing all that I do now, yes."

I was silent for a moment as I thought. "Mom?"

She looked at me.

"Brian is innocent," I whispered. "We can't let him be charged with murder."

Tears filled her eyes. "It's not that easy. We can't just march in there and tell them he didn't do it."

"Why?" I asked quietly, getting angry. I don't know what made me hopeful a moment ago that she'd help me help him, but all hope was lost now. The look in her eyes told me there would be no helping him.

"I don't want to tell you. I don't want you more worried than you already are."

"Just tell me. I can handle it."

She looked over her shoulder, and then at me again. "I lied, I did have contact with someone he worked with," she whispered. "Two days ago, a man called Jerome's phone. I answered it, and when I told him Jerome was missing, he told me he had already heard and he was calling to talk to me."

"What'd he say?" I asked quietly.

"He gave me very clear orders." She absentmindedly rubbed her arm as she got lost in thought and stopped speaking.

"Mom," I said, trying to get her to continue.

"Jorja, there are things you should know and things you shouldn't. The more you know, the more danger you're in. Just please know that I cannot and will not speak a word of who really killed those boys' mother. Your brother, even though he didn't kill her, still drove your father there. He did nothing to stop him. He will still be in trouble for assisting with the murder."

"He didn't have a choice," I almost shouted. "Jerome gave him no choice. Brian had to work for the family!"

"Lower your voice," she said sternly. "Our best strategy is to remain calm, and if you want us both to make it out of this alive, you'll leave the situation with your brother alone."

"What do you know about the tunnels?" I asked quietly.

That rendered her speechless.

"Mom, what do you know about them?" I repeated.

"Do not go looking for them. Do you understand me?"

"They're here in Grove, aren't they?"

"They're everywhere," she whispered. "Jorja Bonovich, so help me, if you go looking for them ..." The fear in her eyes made me rethink that mission, but only momentarily.

"I won't if you tell me what they're used for."

"No. You need to stay out of—"

"I will tell Grandfather I know I'm not Jerome's daughter."

She kept her eyes on mine, and I could tell she was trying to call my bluff. I didn't waver. "Transporting," she said, sounding defeated, "and that's all you need to know. There is constant traffic in them. No place for a teenage girl who knows nothing about the severity of snooping." When she looked at the floor, I knew right then that that traffic was flowing beneath the house at this very moment. Her eyes met mine again, pleading with me. "This is dangerous."

"It all is. Our entire life has been dangerous. I don't understand why you would even bring kids into a life like this. It's selfish."

"Do not question my motives. I am your mother, and I love you more than anything in the entire world. Just because I brought you into a family of villains doesn't mean I don't have the right to be a mother."

I wouldn't apologize for what I said, even if I cared that I upset her. It was the truth. I didn't ask to be here. I didn't ask to live in this hell. This life caused me to murder someone. People I cared about lost their mother to this life.

"Unless you've changed your mind and you're going to let me come home, I'd like to be alone now." I wrapped my arms around myself and walked to the large doors that led out to a balcony. I stared into the night instead of looking at my mother when she spoke.

"I love you, Jorja."

Tears burned my eyes. "I love you, too," I said, without looking at her.

When I heard the door open and close, I relaxed a little. I stepped onto the balcony and enjoyed the cold on my skin. It made me focus solely on it instead of everything else.

CHAPTER ELEVEN

Rush

"She won't stop texting me," Toby said from the other side of the living room. He sat in the recliner, and I lay on the couch. We had a movie going, but neither of us were really paying attention.

Jena had been texting him nonstop once he was added to the group chat and she was able to get his number. Toby hated attention, but I thought it would be good for him. All he did was stay home, read, or do homework.

"Tell her to stop texting then," I said, laughing.

"But I don't want to be mean."

I laughed some more. "What is she saying?"

"It's only been ten minutes, and I already know her favorite color, favorite food, favorite band, smell, and that she can say the alphabet backwards." The more I laughed, the deeper he frowned. "It's not funny. I didn't even ask her those things. All I said was hi back and then she just started sending text after text. Is she always this bouncy?"

"I've never heard Jena described as bouncy before."

"Like a damn bouncy ball with the facts she's throwing out there about herself." He groaned when his phone dinged three more times. "Favorite sport, favorite shoe brand, favorite sock brand ..." He scratched his head. "Sock brand? Seriously?" When the phone dinged two more times, he dropped it, threw his hands up, and said, "Make it stop!"

I was laughing so hard it was difficult to breathe.

My laughter faded when I heard the front door open and close. Toby looked at me when we heard Dad's voice calling our names.

"In here," Toby called out as he picked up his phone. I watched as he powered it off.

Dad walked into the room and looked at us. "Where's the remote? I caught wind they were going to be interviewing Jorja and the rest of the family tonight."

I quickly sat up and grabbed the remote from the coffee table and tossed it to Dad. He changed it to the local news. I could feel my heart beating in my throat when I saw Jorja on the screen. Alongside her was her mom and who I assumed were the grandparents she was staying with. Jorja kept her eyes on the floor as her grandfather spoke.

"We are eagerly looking for any information anyone has on my son, Jerome Bonovich. There is a reward of fifty-thousand dollars for his safe return. Please, if you have any information at all, let the authorities know. Our hearts are desperate for answers."

The news presenter asked if anyone else would like to speak, and no one spoke up. Not right away, anyway. Jorja looked up, and when her eyes found the camera, it felt like she was staring straight at me. I could see a hint of something peculiar in her eyes when she interrupted the presenter as he was closing to tell him she had something to say. Her mother and grandparents, wide eyed, stared at her as she made her way to the microphone.

"We believe Brian Bonovich, my brother, is innocent, and we will also be searching for—" Her mother grabbed her by the arm and started to pull her away, effectively ending her speech.

The news changed quickly to a commercial.

"Oh, shit," Dad mumbled as he sat down slowly on the couch next to me.

What was she thinking? It was obvious that it wasn't a part of the planned speech.

Dad rubbed his forehead. "This isn't good. This isn't good at all."

"Why?" Toby asked. "What just happened?"

"The Bonoviches have framed Brian for the death of your mother for a reason. Jorja just started a war within her own family."

Toby paled. "They won't hurt her, will they?"

"That family is capable of anything." Dad cursed a few times. "That girl isn't stupid. She knows exactly what she's doing."

Did she, though? Or did she just do that on a whim? I needed a way to talk to her. She probably just put a million targets on her back. I looked at Toby and noticed how lost in thought he was. I knew what I had to do.

"Dad," I said nervously. When he looked at me, I continued, "I'm going to tell what I saw."

"Rush, you're—"

"I'm going to tell," I said with more sureness. "It's my narrative to tell, not anyone else's. If Jorja thinks it's important for everyone to know that her brother is innocent, then I'm going to back her up and confirm what she is saying is true."

Dad shook his head adamantly. "No."

"Set up an interview with an attorney."

"Rush," Toby interjected, "think about this."

"I don't have to. I'm doing it with or without support."

Dad sighed heavily. "Give me until the end of the week to hire an attorney."

I nodded.

CHAPTER TWELVE

Toby

School felt unnecessary with everything going on. I don't know why I felt like the world should stop spinning, but it sure as hell didn't feel right going through the normal motions of each day. Jorja was in attendance, even though I had expected her not to be after her news debut. It was crazy how overnight it all blew up into the biggest national news story headline. Everyone was talking about it, and new reporters lined the front of the school like she was famous. I guess she *was* famous.

I wrote her a letter and gave it to Becca to get to her this morning. It was after lunch and Becca told me she'd meet me by my locker if she wrote back. Waiting for her felt like an eternity. Maybe Jorja didn't write

back, though. My worries were silenced when I saw
Becca walking toward me—parting the crowd like the
Red Sea. Like Jorja, she had a presence about her.
The whole group did.

She quickly handed me the letter. "She made me
promise I'd tell you to burn the letter after you read it.
She would be doing the same with yours."

"Did you read it?"

Becca laughed. "Tempting, but no. She made me
swear I wouldn't." Becca flipped her hair over her
shoulder. "I have a question, Tobias."

"Yeah?" I stuck the note in my back pocket.

"What are your intentions with Jorja?"

"What do you mean?"

She laughed. "I mean, do you like her?"

"I need to get to class, and so do you." I started
walking away.

"I always find things out, Tobias!" she called after
me.

As soon as I made it to the classroom and was
seated, I took the letter out to read it.

Toby,

*I want you and Rush to meet me at the graveyard
we own at midnight tonight. I have a plan.*

-Jorja

She didn't comment on anything I said in my
letter. Maybe the part where she said she has a plan is

her response. I told her Rush planned on going to the cops about what he saw. I told her I was worried about her. I told her I missed her.

I folded the paper and put it into my coat pocket. I'd burn it later.

As I walked down the hall, an announcement came over the intercom:

Tobias and Rush True are needed to the office with their belongings.

I frowned, unsure of why we were needed, and headed toward the office.

When I walked in, I saw Rush had beaten me there. There were two men in suits and FBI badges waiting for us. I looked at Rush who never took his eyes off them. We were led into a large conference room, where the taller man with dark skin shut the door and stood by it. The other man looked old with graying hair, and he instructed us to sit.

"What's going on?" I asked, setting my backpack on the floor next to the chair.

Rush slowly took a seat next to me and set his bag by mine.

"I'm Agent Owens and," he motioned toward the agent by the door, "this is Agent Jones. We have a few questions and were given permission by your father to speak to you here." At that moment, Dad was let into the room.

Rush and I both looked at him.

"Answer any questions they have honestly," Dad instructed as he took a seat across from us.

The questions came rolling in, and I was thankful for twin intuition, because Rush and I stuck to the same lie about where we were and what we knew about Jerome missing.

"I hope Dad stays asleep," Rush whispered while we waited in the thickest part of the woods near the graveyard. From our standpoint, we would be able to see when Jorja walked up but were still hidden from others.

"There she is," I said as I pushed off the tree I was leaning against.

We remained quiet as we walked out of the woods and into the clearing. When Jorja saw us, she picked up her pace. When she was close enough, she reached out and grabbed both of us into a hug.

"I was so scared you wouldn't be here. Did you burn the letter?" she asked me.

I nodded. "Did you burn yours?"

She nodded.

I explained everything to Rush on the way there so he wouldn't be over analyzing things.

"How'd you get out of your grandparents' house?" Rush asked.

"I found their secret exit. I've been snooping, and I've found out a lot of things." She looked at Rush seriously. "You're not telling a damn person you saw Jerome kill your mother. Got it?"

"But—"

"But nothing. I have a plan."

"Why'd you tell everyone on live television Brian is innocent then?" he challenged her.

"Because I need the media following this. I need as many people interested and invested in the case so when I bring this family to their knees, the entire world is watching." The fire in her eyes made it clear she wasn't playing games. She was serious.

"Why meet here?" I asked.

"Because—" she started walking as she continued to speak "—there is a grave here, if my findings are correct, that is actually a secret entrance to tunnels that run underground. There are some under my grandparents' home, but I haven't found them yet." She pulled a small piece of paper from her back pocket. "These are the coordinates."

Rush and I both walked over to her, and she showed us the paper. Neither of us understood the numbers, but she did. We followed her as she walked through the graves, backtracking her steps a few times, before we finally made it to a grave that was slightly larger than the others. It was next to a brick storage building that looked more like a mini house.

Jorja looked at the grave and then at the building. "It's not the grave." She tried to open the door to the building, but it was locked. She pulled a bobby pin from her pocket and started working on picking the lock. "If this doesn't work, I'll need to go to the funeral home to look for the key."

"What is the plan?" I asked, looking around us, scanning the perimeter. Anyone could be out here watching us right now.

"To bring down the Bonoviches. Even if I go down with them," she said, matter-of-factly.

Rush chuckled. "We know that, but what is the actual plan to do so?"

She cursed when she couldn't get the lock to open. "I'm planning as I go." She put the bobby pin into her pocket and looked at me and my brother. "I need to go to the funeral home."

"Why are we here?" I asked.

"I wanted to see you both, and I wanted you to know that I'm going to do whatever it takes to bring justice for your mother's death and everyone else who has been negatively impacted by Jerome and this family. I'm not asking for your help; I just want you both to know."

"I'll help," Rush said quickly. "Whatever you need, I'll help."

Jorja smiled softly. "Thank you, but you don't have to."

"But we want to," I interjected with a grin. "And all of your friends want to help too. You can't do it alone."

"They want to help?" She looked so confused. "What do they know?"

"Only what everyone knows. That'd be up to you to tell them anything else," Rush said as he moved closer to her. "You have an army. Small, but an army nevertheless."

"Thank you," she said, looking at the both of us.

"How long will you be with your grandparents?" I asked.

She shrugged. "No clue. We need to go to the funeral home and look for the key." She looked at our vehicles. "I should go alone, though. You two go home. Meet back here again, tomorrow night, same time?"

"Are you sure going alone is safe?" I asked.

"I know the ins and outs of that place. I know what I'm looking for. The less the better. I'll be fine."

Her tone was playful, trying to brush off my worry, but I could see in her eyes that she was scared. But if I'd learned anything about Jorja, it's that she is stubborn, and no matter how much I begged her to let us go with her, she wouldn't do it. Regardless, I suggested it anyway.

"I don't think you should be doing any of it alone. It's dangerous. Let us come with you."

Rush looked at me and then at her. "He's right, Jorja. Let us come."

She shook her head, just as I suspected. "No. I promise, I'll be fine." When we continued to look at her skeptically, she sighed. "I'm serious. You're not coming."

We agreed, but I knew we'd follow her anyway.

CHAPTER THIRTEEN

Jorja

When I made it inside the funeral home, I turned off the security system. The keys to the graveyard were on a wall, labeled, in the main office. I started scanning them, predicting that the key in particular would be extremely hard to find. If my findings were correct, then the key would be hidden due to the fact that it led to the tunnels.

It wouldn't be on the wall.

Jerome was smarter than that.

I started going through a drawer when I heard a sound. I sighed heavily. "Toby, Rush ... I told you not—" When the footsteps were behind me, I turned to see my sister. "Olivia?"

"Breathe," she said as she took notice of my apparent state of panic.

Did I hug her? Cry? Yell at her for leaving us? Leaving me.

"Don't say a word. Just listen. Okay?"

I nodded, my heart threatening to escape my chest. I stayed seated in the chair but closed the drawer.

"I'm on the same mission as you. Several strides ahead, as a matter of fact. You need help. This isn't something that can be done alone. They're watching. They're probably watching now."

"But no one has known where you are."

She put her fingers to lips. "I said no talking."

I closed my mouth tight, my entire body trembling. I couldn't believe this was happening. Here was Olivia, my estranged sister. The one whose room was demolished and turned into a suite for me. The one who haunted my memories and left me questioning so many things.

"They have known, Jorja. They have known but didn't tell because they wanted to find me and end me. I'm done running. I'm here. I will lay low, but I'm sick of what this family is doing and has done. When I found out that you learned Jerome wasn't your real father, I knew I had to find a way back here. That things could really start happening to bring this family down. Then when I saw you and your friends dump him in the river, I knew then that I wouldn't have to fight alone."

I swallowed hard—my hands turned clammy at the revelation that me and the boys weren't alone that night. "How'd you see?"

"I didn't see you actually hurl his body over the edge, though it would have been extremely satisfying ..." She smiled at the thought. "But I did see you take off on the boat, and when you returned, the body was no longer there. How'd it feel? Tossing that monster into the water to rot?"

"I only felt relief until I got home and started thinking about it all. That's the thing ... I don't think it solved anything."

"It didn't solve anything but ignited the fire to burn this family."

Had she been inside my head? Her thoughts aligning with mine comforted me in an odd way. "I know about the tunnels."

"I haven't found the key. I've looked everywhere. Is that why you're here?"

I nodded.

"It's not here. I think it's at the house. In the study."

I still couldn't believe I was actually talking to my sister. Here in the flesh. "Olivia?" I narrowed my eyes in her direction. "Where have you been?"

"Here. There. Everywhere."

"Why did you run from me at the hospital?"

"We couldn't talk in public like that. I snuck in to see Brian."

Tears filled my eyes. My brother. I missed him so much. "Is he okay?"

"He was up and talking. I've seen him a lot over the years, actually."

That revelation hurt. Gutted me. "Why not me?" I said, angry. My outburst was warranted, whether she agreed or not. "You just abandoned me!"

"You were young," she cried.

"But not naive to your disappearance. The family treated your name as if it were sin. I wasn't allowed to ask questions. They demolished your room. I ..."

I started to sob and hated myself for it. I wanted to be strong and numb to it all, but I couldn't keep that facade up anymore. I didn't even know who I was. By blood, I was an Ellison and part my mother's—a Gavin. By raising, I was a Bonovich. I didn't want to be either. Since finding out I was part Ellison, the man who was my father never reached out. Peter was my half-brother; no word from him either. He didn't even come to school anymore.

Olivia came over and wrapped me in her arms. I held onto her and cried. She cried, too. I needed to let the tears flow. Years of pent-up anger and confusion came flooding out, and as much as I hated the vulnerability, it felt good.

When I finally calmed down, I sat up and looked at my sister.

She wiped her eyes on her sleeve and smiled a little. "You should know," she said, "those boys are out there waiting on you. Care to tell me what's going on?"

I laughed. "Of course they are, and what do you mean?"

"You know exactly what I mean. They both have it bad for you."

"That's not what's important right now. They're some of my best friends. I can count on them."

"They're good people. The Trues have always been, pun unintended, but hilarious, truly wonderful."

That made me laugh out loud. "How do you know?"

"I've been watching. Doing my research. I didn't abandon you, Jorja; I have kept a close watch and was ready to step in as soon as I saw you needed me. You're strong."

I wiped my eyes on the back of my hand. "I don't look so strong right now."

"Yes, you do. You're sitting in the funeral home looking for answers. It's risky, but you're here."

"Does Mom know you're here?"

She shook her head. "We need to talk about Mom. She can't be trusted. She loves us, but she loves money more. She will always choose the business over us. She'll make you think her decisions are to protect you, but they are really to protect her fortune."

I knew that but never wanted to fully admit it. I felt like I was going to be sick. This was too much. "Brian is innocent."

"He is, but he's tired. He doesn't want to fight anymore. We were actually working together, we had a plan, but then—"

"I screwed it up, didn't I?"

She smiled softly. "To be fair, you didn't know what we were doing, so you had no idea your decisions could interfere with ours."

"We should get out of here. These drug runs happen late, and if they are making a stop today, we need to be gone."

"Where are you staying?"

"I'm not going to tell you. Not yet."

I wanted to protest, but it was probably for the best. "I'm digging for any information I can find about our grandparents' house. Your grandparents' ... Jerome's parent's ..."

"It's okay to call them your grandparents, too. Blood or not, this is the family that raised you."

"They don't know I'm not blood."

She scoffed. "I'm sure they don't. The family is full of hidden truths. We should—" Olivia looked over her shoulder, and when I looked past her, I saw a shadow of someone. When they came into view, I grabbed Olivia's arm.

Jerome.

It can't—

A gunshot sounded before we could react, and before I could register anything, I felt the deep pain and then felt the blood begin to pour from my right side. I started to stumble forward when Olivia caught me, then a second gunshot filled the air, and Olivia pulled me onto the floor behind the desk with her. What happened next was all a blur before my sister's face faded into darkness.

CHAPTER FOURTEEN

Rush

Dad came running into the waiting room. "Have you two lost your damn minds?" he yelled. He wasn't in uniform; tonight he was off, and we had snuck out once he was asleep.

"Right now isn't a good time to be yelling at us," Toby snapped as he motioned his hands around the waiting room. People were watching.

"I don't give a damn who hears me! What were you two doing out? I told you to leave that girl alone!"

I didn't know if he was being serious or if he was trying to put on a show for everyone. Either way, it was believable. "She was shot. Twice possibly. We heard two gunshots," I added.

"Did you see anyone else?" he asked, entering officer mode. As he eyed me up and down, a perplexed gaze fixated on my bare chest. "And why aren't you wearing a shirt?"

"No one else was there that we know of," Toby said. "It's all a blur now. I broke the glass doors to get inside, and she was passed out ... blood everywhere. Rush gave me his shirt, and I applied pressure but there was so much." Toby started to pale as he looked at the blood on his hands.

I had blood all over me too, but I refused to look. I was the one who carried her out and met the medics.

"Is she okay?" Dad asked, looking at the both of us.

Toby sat slowly in a chair. He started to speak but couldn't. Tears filled his eyes, and he looked down at the floor.

"We don't know," my voice was strained, and tears started to fall. "We don't know," I said again, the blur of everything becoming a brick of reality hitting me head on. Everything felt heavy. I took a seat next to my brother.

Dad pulled his wallet from his back pocket. I saw him fumble to get his ID out. He walked over to the receptionist and held it up. "Officer True. Let me back there."

She nodded, and the doors opened.

"I never saw anyone go in the funeral home, did you?" I asked, my voice low. I wiped the tears from my cheeks.

Toby stared at his blood-stained hands. "No," he said quietly. He looked at me. "We should've never let her go."

"We couldn't have stopped her."

"She needs people that will stop her, Rush. Look at this! Look at us!" He held up his hands full of her blood. "We might lose her tonight!"

I felt like I was going to be sick. "We won't lose her."

"You sure about that? This is all your fault. And Peter's. If you all would have never made that stupid plan—"

"I stopped the plan! Peter kept it going! This is old news. We aren't rehashing it."

"You orchestrated it from the beginning, Rush! You were dead set on ending that family until you fell for her! She could still be living safely in her home without all the revelations that have caused her to go looking for answers!"

"That's not fair. You can't blame me." I felt like I couldn't breathe. I knew he was angry and scared, but, surely, he didn't mean the things he was saying. But I also knew my brother. He never struggled with honesty. "Where is this coming from? I thought we were past this."

"Well, now the girl we are falling for is in there fighting for her damn life!"

We.

He said *we.*

I raised a brow. "You're falling for her?"

He scoffed. "You knew that, yet you're okay watching me suffer in silence for the sake of your feelings. I promised I'd never interfere, and I won't. Not unless she wants me to."

"Are we seriously having this conversation right now while she's in a room bleeding to death?"

He shrugged. "What does it matter, Rush? It'd come out sooner or later. If something happens to her, I will never forgive you."

"That's not fair!"

"What's not fair is her possibly dying tonight." He stood. "I need some air." With that, he walked out of the waiting room.

I put my head in my hands and tried to ignore the eyes of the others in the room. The sound of coughing and children crying was too much. Going outside for some air would be nice, but I couldn't stand to be next to my brother right now. How dare he say the things he did in a moment like this. It wasn't my fault. Toby was just scared and couldn't have meant that if he were in his right mind. However, the more I tried to convince myself it wasn't my fault, maybe it was. Maybe Toby was right.

Peter putting heat on her family, the plan that was originally mine in vengeance of my mother's death, is the ball that set this all into motion. Jorja deserved to know the complete truth about her family, but maybe not knowing everything would've been safer. Maybe we aren't meant to know the truth and that's why lies and deception exist. In this case, it could've saved her life.

CHAPTER FIFTEEN

Toby

I broke down, and I didn't want anyone to see it.

I know the things I said to my brother were hurtful, and I wasn't sure if I meant all of it. Jorja would've eventually wanted answers regardless of my brother and Peter's involvement. Or would she have? Maybe she wouldn't be as hungry for them if no one challenged her family the way Peter did.

It all made sense why Peter did it, though. Rush and Peter both had reasons to put her family through hell. Our mother's death, Peter found out Jorja was his sister and that her family kept her from him. I can't imagine the pain her real father felt. I'm sure they made him keep quiet and he had to watch her grow up keeping that secret. Maybe that's why they lived so close to them. So he *could* watch her grow up. Maybe it was an agreement they had. The layers of Jorja's life and the depths of the secrets were never ending.

I gained control of my emotions and used the bottom of my blood-stained shirt to wipe my eyes. My hands trembled as I fought with God to save her. This couldn't be the way it was supposed to end.

I pressed my back against the brick wall and closed my eyes, trying to calm myself down. When I heard a lot of voices and a car door shutting, I peered around the corner to see reporters, her grandparents, and her mother being escorted inside.

I went inside so Rush wouldn't have to deal with it alone.

Rush was being bombarded by reporters and her family was guarded by police on the other side of the waiting room. I didn't see her mother, so I assumed she was already back with Jorja. I pushed through the reporters to make my way to Rush.

"Is that Jorja Bonovich's blood you're covered in?" a male reporter asked, shoving a microphone in my face. The bright lights from flashes and a video camera came into view as I blinked.

I didn't answer, I grabbed my brother's arm, and we pushed through until we made it outside. We were being followed, yelled at, and questioned. I told him not to respond as we hurried to my truck. The last thing I wanted to do was leave Jorja, but there was no way they'd let us in to see her.

Once inside the truck and the doors were locked, Rush looked at me. "We can't leave. We can't leave her."

I looked at the reporters swarming the truck. "What about them?"

"They'll leave eventually, right?"

"I don't know," I answered, taking notice of how puffy his eyes were.

The reporters took notice of something, or rather, someone, else. They hurried in that direction and my mouth fell open. "Rush," I said, pointing toward the Ellisons walking in, trailed by the media.

"This isn't good," he started to get out, but I stopped him.

"We will cause more harm than good in there. Trust me, I want to be in there as badly as you do, but there's no way we'll get to see her right now. Let's just wait on Dad."

I sent Dad a quick text to let him know we went out to my truck. I figured it'd be a while before we heard from him, so I cranked the trunk, turned on the heat, and laid my head against the window. Rush did the same, and it wasn't long before we both fell asleep.

I jerked awake when there was a knock on my window. Dad stood there, motioning for me to roll down the window. The sun was starting to come up, casting an orange hue over the parking lot. I tapped Rush's shoulder to wake him.

I rubbed my neck. "How is she?"

Exhaustion invaded Dad's eyes. "Resting. She's going to be fine."

"Can we see her?" I asked.

"You both go home and get cleaned up. I'll try to pull some strings to get you both in there. Right now, her grandparents and her mother are with her. I'll text when the coast is clear."

I nodded. "Thank you, Dad."

"Don't thank me just yet. You're both in a shit-ton of trouble. When you come back to town, I need you to bring my uniform. I'm sticking around here to help with the media, and we have another search going out today for Jerome Bonovich."

"Is she talking yet or still asleep?" Rush asked.

"She's been in and out but hasn't said a word to anyone. She wouldn't answer any of my questions, either."

I remembered I was still covered in her blood. "We'll get cleaned up and wait on your call."

He nodded. "Okay, and you'll both have to give your report of what happened at some point today."

"Yes, sir," Rush and I said in unison.

"You boys be careful. Love you."

After telling him we loved him too, I put the truck in reverse and headed home.

CHAPTER SIXTEEN

Jorja

"Your job is to sit still and look pretty. You're not going to go snooping for anything else, you got it?" Grandmother said as she sat next to the hospital bed. My mother was pacing the room, agreeing with every word.

I kept my eyes shut and focused on keeping my breathing even. As soon as my grandfather had left earlier to handle "business", my grandmother and mother took advantage of telling me exactly how Bonovich women would react. I could feel myself growing more and more fed up as she continued to tell me what I would do. Knowing Edward Ellison, my true father, was here to see me and speak to me set a new fire in my veins. At first, I wasn't sure why he would want to see me now, or ever, for that matter, but learning things about this family made me question everything any of them have ever told me. I wanted to hear what he had to say. I wanted to hear all the stories so I could figure out which one to believe. That's if that's what he wants to talk to me about at all.

I opened my eyes to glare at my grandmother. Why was I even allowing myself to refer to my grandfather and her as my grandparents? Olivia said it was fine, but it wasn't. I didn't want to associate myself with them any longer. Henrietta and Jacob from here on out.

"Are you aware of your duties to this family, child?"

"Let Edward Ellison in," I demanded. The first words I uttered since waking up after being shot.

"Jorja—"

I cut my mother off. "Let him in."

"He is not welcome in—"

This time I screamed as loud as I could, cutting off Henrietta. "He's my father! Let him in!"

With the press here, everyone learned the truth about who my father was on live television. I watched as Edward Ellison spoke out about my true parentage on the five o'clock news, the contract between Jerome, my mother, and him in his shaking hands for proof. I wasn't sure exactly what prompted him to announce it to the media like that, but maybe it was my near-death experience that made him not want to go to the grave with his secret after all.

"He's a possible suspect now, Jorja! They are going to be bringing him in for questioning. He might've done something to Jerome!" My mother was sobbing now. "It makes sense. He got rid of him so Jerome was no longer a threat to him."

"I said let him in!" The force it took to be able to raise my voice hurt. I clenched my teeth in pain, sweat forming on my brow. The morphine drip wasn't even touching the pain radiating from my right hip.

I wished my sister were with me. I had no idea where she went or if she had been shot too. There were two gunshots. The thought of her leaving me there to die hurt and made me wonder if I could really trust her. Flashes of Jerome shooting me invaded my memories of the night before, and I had to keep pushing them away because he was *dead*. It couldn't have been him. The hysteria from being shot had to have induced hallucinations.

"I want you both out and to let him in. I have rights that not even you are powerful enough to deny me."

My mother looked defeated and tired. "We'll go get him, but this will be the only time he is allowed to speak to you," she said flatly.

Henrietta pointed her bony frail finger at me. "This conversation isn't over. You will obey."

I didn't respond. I only waited for her to get the hint and leave.

They both left, and it gave me a moment to catch my breath and prepare myself for who would come through that door next. I carefully orchestrated questions in my mind that I hoped the pain meds wouldn't make me forget.

When the door opened again, the man who shared my eyes walked in. He shut the door behind him and stood at the foot of the bed. He looked so nervous, but who could blame him? Thankfully, I had morphine to take some of the edge off, but even I felt like I needed to run.

"They say you're going to be alright."

I nodded.

"I'm sorry you found out who I am the way you did." He put his hands into his jean pockets.

"I was never supposed to find out." I paid attention to his facial expressions, trying to make sure I was observing the difference between a truth and a lie, but that was hard to do with someone you don't really know.

"That's not because I didn't want you to know. It was an agreement."

"I saw you have a copy of the contract with you. Can I see it?"

He reached inside his coat and pulled out an envelope. "I figured you'd want to." He handed it to me. "The specifics of what he would do to my family if I broke it was strategically left out of there but delivered verbally."

I was so weak that the paper felt like a brick. Noticing my struggle, he took it and opened it for me.

This Agreement, entered into between the Bonovich Family ("Family A") and the Ellison Family ("Family B"), aims to prevent any interference by Edward Ellison, in the life of Jorja Bonovich, a minor child of Family A. Family B, including Edward Ellison and his family members, agrees not to interfere directly or indirectly with Jorja's life, upbringing, or affairs. In the event of any violation, Family A reserves the right to take necessary actions to ensure Jorja's safety and well-being, including legal recourse. Both parties agree to maintain the confidentiality of this Agreement, which shall remain effective indefinitely, governed by the laws of the jurisdiction, until terminated by mutual agreement or by a court of competent jurisdiction.

Seeing it with my own eyes hurt worse than I had expected. I knew it, but seeing it and being given to me by the man who shared my blood, made it concrete. Made it feel real. I gently pushed it away.

"What now?" I asked quietly.

"You tell me, Jorja. You're old enough to decide how you want to proceed. I will understand if you don't want a relationship with me."

I kept my eyes on him, noticing for the first time how much I favored him. I shook my head and tears burned my eyes. "You're a junkie. The only reason I exist is because you needed a fix that my supposed father could offer, and he gave you bad drugs and wronged you financially. My mother was a wager for you to use to get another sick fix from. A bad deal made right. You got her pregnant on purpose! Everyone around me is a monster." I was crying harder, and while being vulnerable wasn't something I wanted to be in front of this man, I couldn't help it. I was exhausted.

He looked stunned. Hurt, maybe. I was too drugged up and in pain to know for sure.

"Is that what you were told?"

I nodded.

"And you believed that?"

I shrugged. "I don't know what to believe anymore."

"None of that is true, Jorja," he said, struggling to speak.

"And why would I believe anything you say?"

"Because I'm not them," his voice cracked. "And I didn't hurt Jerome. I know they think I did, but I didn't."

Of course he didn't. I did.

A nurse walked in, and I looked at the clock. Every hour they came in to check my vitals. Edward Ellison put the contract back into the inner pocket of his coat. The nurse asked him to step out because they needed to check my wound. I almost told her to let him stay so he could see what happened and let it sink into his bones with just a glimpse of what it meant to be a Bonovich. However I ended up in this world, whichever truth was real, I still could've been killed last night. I didn't ask for this, but I would end it.

I closed my eyes when he left the room and let the nurses do their job. They told me the doctor would be in soon to discuss surgery, which immediately sent me into a panic.

"Surgery?" My breathing picked up. "No one said anything about surgery." I should've known. The pain was unbearable, and I wasn't allowed to walk yet. Even if I wanted to, I couldn't. There was a bullet lodged in my hip bone. That part I remembered and felt.

"When you came in, we had to get you stable and stop the bleeding. You were in-and-out of sleep during the MRI. The doctor will explain it further. He should be in at any moment."

I hissed in pain as she changed the dressing on my hip. I closed my eyes and waited. When I opened them, I noticed the doctor walking in. Tears from the pain slid down my cheeks.

"Miss Bonovich, I'm Doctor Oliver, and we will be performing surgery later today." He looked young but had a way about him that made me feel like he could be trusted.

"Just call me Jorja, please."

His smile was kind and warm. "Jorja, do you know why you're here?"

"I was shot in my hip."

He nodded. "According to the MRI, you have what we call a pertrochanteric fracture. This type of fracture is very complex because the bone is most likely broken into multiple pieces. While in there, I will need to repair the bone and assess and address any other damage to nearby tissues and possible organs from the injury. That means repairing or removing damaged tissue to be sure everything heals as it should."

I swallowed hard. "And recovery?"

He set his clipboard on the counter. "It'll involve staying in the hospital a few days for monitoring and to help manage your pain. You can expect physical therapy in your near future to regain strength and mobility to your hip joint. You're in good hands here. Your recovery is our top priority."

I thought about cheer and how it would affect me going to college on a cheer scholarship. That's only if, one day, I can pursue dreams like that. "Can I still cheer?"

"It's very possible, but it will depend on your personal recovery. It can be different for everyone." He smiled again. "Let's just take this one day at a time right now."

I nodded and closed my eyes again. The pain and nerves were making me nauseous. "Let's just get it over with."

"Get some rest, and I'll see you in surgery."

I opened my eyes to watch him and the nurse leave the room. I tried to move a little, but it was impossible. It hurt too much. I was about to wallow in my own pity until I realized something. Brian was in the hospital—if he hadn't been released yet—and with the condition he was in, surely they hadn't let him go yet. If I could somehow get the guys back here to see me, I could have them get a message to him. Despite the pain, I was still able to work out a plan.

CHAPTER SEVENTEEN

Rush

Just as Dad promised, he was able to sneak us in to see Jorja. Her family had gone for the night, and typically visitors weren't allowed at this hour, but Dad knew enough people that respected him, and they were able to make it happen.

Toby and I didn't go in through the front, but through the back where nurses and doctors entered the building. When we made it to her room, Dad looked at the both of us.

"She's in a lot of pain and in and out of sleep. They said this was normal with how long she had to be asleep during surgery mixed with the pain meds."

She was sound asleep when we entered the room. Even hurt, she looked flawless. I tried to push my jealousy aside when her eyes opened slowly and they settled on Toby. She blinked a few times and went to move but quickly stopped when she whimpered in pain.

"Don't move. Just rest," Toby said quietly.

I noticed two chairs already placed on either side of her bed. I looked at Dad as he gave me and Toby a slight nod.

"I'll be standing outside the door to stand guard. You boys have an hour."

We both thanked him, and after he left the room and shut the door, Toby and I each sat in a chair.

Her eyes finally found me, and she smiled softly. "How'd you get in?" she asked sleepily.

"It pays being a cop's son," I said, smiling back. I took her hand that didn't have an IV in it. I rubbed my thumb gently over the back of her hand. "How are you feeling?"

"It hurts," she whispered. "So much."

"Dad explained what all they had to do," Toby said from the other side of the bed.

"Yeah, it wasn't nearly as bad as they thought it would be, so that's good." She spoke slowly and yawned. "I wish I could stay awake. The nightmares won't stop." Her eyes closed again, and her grip on my hand loosened. She forced herself awake again and looked at me, gripping my hand tightly again. "Brian. He's here. Go find him. Tell him what happened."

"Jorja, that won't be easy. We barely got in to see you," I said carefully. I didn't want to upset her, but it was the truth.

"Tell your dad everything. I trust him," she said, keeping her eyes on mine. She turned her head to look at Toby. "Tell him, okay? We need his help."

"*Everything?*" Toby asked.

She nodded slowly, and her eyes started to close.

"Maybe we should wait until she's not so out of it," I mentioned, and she opened her eyes long enough to shoot me an evil look.

"Tell him," she said again. "I know he'll help us."

I looked at Toby and knew he agreed with me. She wasn't in her right mind to be making that kind of decision.

"Okay, Jorja. We'll talk to him," Toby lied. He was just trying to pacify her.

"I ..." She was really struggling to stay awake now. "I saw him."

"Who?" I asked.

"Olivia was there." Jorja's eyes remained closed. "And ... Jerome."

Impossible.

He was dead.

I saw his lifeless body.

Toby looked at me, eyes wide. He gently rubbed her arm. "Get some sleep."

She nodded slowly. "Don't leave me," she begged in a whisper before falling into a deep sleep.

I looked at Toby. "She's talking crazy," I said quietly, but loud enough for him to hear.

"She's on a lot of pain meds. I'm sure she's not thinking straight." He stared at her; his forehead creased with worry. "What if we hadn't been there?"

"The what ifs will haunt us forever if we let them."

He nodded slowly. I noticed his hand was still lightly rubbing her arm. Toby had fallen for her, that was no secret, and it gutted me.

"Let's call a truce," I said, watching him pull his eyes from her and to me.

"A truce?"

"You were right, Jorja isn't a prize to be won. We're her best friends before anything else. If she chooses one of us, we deal with it. I can't lose my brother."

"I told you I won't interfere."

I shook my head. "That's not fair to anyone in this situation. I want what's best for her, and if that's you—" my next words gutted me "—then I will accept it."

"Rush ... she cares for you. I think that's clear."

"Yet she won't fully commit. I haven't wanted to admit to myself, and maybe she hasn't even realized it yet, but I believe you're the reason why."

"Or she's literally going through hell right now and dating is the least of her worries."

I nodded. "Or that."

Toby got lost in thought for a moment. "But if it's not that ... you're sure you wouldn't be mad?"

I laughed. "I promise to suffer in silence."

We didn't say anything the rest of the hour we sat with her. It killed me to let my guard down like that, but seeing her lying in the hospital bed brought an entire new perspective to it all.

CHAPTER EIGHTEEN

Toby

My mind was in a million places since the conversation with my brother. This changed everything. My walls with Jorja were officially down, and it felt exhilarating and scary as hell. I could be the part of me that fell for her.

I asked Dad to find a way for me to see her before school because, despite everything, he still made us go the next day. When I asked him what kind of father made his kids go to school the day after they were involved in a shooting, his response was: "Better get some sleep." But, he still told me he'd get me in early before the family visiting hours opened. Rush said he was going to take his truck to school, so I didn't have to worry about giving him a ride.

Different nurses from the night before snuck me in the back door. Once I made it into Jorja's room, I was surprised to see her fully awake and sitting up. Her smile lit up the whole room when she saw me.

After closing the door behind me, I went over to her and hugged gently. "Morning."

"How'd you get in?"

I sat in the chair beside her bed. "The same way we did last night."

"You were here last night?"

My smile faded a little. "Yeah, you don't remember? Rush and I were both here."

She shook her head. "No."

"You were in and out of sleep, but you talked to us a little."

She scrunched her nose. "Did I say anything embarrassing?"

I chuckled. "No, but you said some concerning things. I'm sure it was just the meds and the sleepiness."

"What'd I say?"

"You said you saw your sister and Jerome at the funeral home, and you asked us to tell our dad everything."

She paled. "Did you tell him? And I said what I said because I did see them. Did I tell anyone else that?" I could see the panic filling her eyes.

I shook my head. "I don't think so." I leaned forward so I was closer to her. "Olivia may have been there, Jorja, but Jerome is dead. And no. We didn't tell him."

She relaxed a little but not fully. "I saw him, Toby. I know I did."

"Before or after you were shot?"

"After, but—"

"The pain and the shock could've caused you to see things. He's dead," I said, whispering the last part.

"I know I sound crazy. I know what you're saying, but I'm telling you, he was there. I don't know if Olivia is okay ... She may have been shot, too."

I grabbed her hand when tears started to fall. "Let's not worry about any of that right now. You need to focus on getting better."

"How can I not worry about it?"

I didn't have an answer for her because I was worried too. "I don't know."

She closed her eyes as tears fell. "I'm scared."

"We'll figure it all out. Right now—"

She opened her eyes and looked at me. "I know ... focus on getting better." She put her head back against the pillow with a dramatic sigh. "They said they're going to let me start walking today. With help, of course."

"Just take it easy. I know how stubborn you are."

That initiated a smile, but it didn't last long. "Did I say anything else concerning last night?"

"You asked us to find a way to see Brian, but I don't know how we will. Your friends are trying to figure out a way, though."

"They are?"

At that moment, I knew she had no idea about the meeting we all had at the lake. For some reason, I assumed Becca or someone would have told her. "You didn't know?"

She shook her head. "But you're going to tell me everything."

I rubbed my forehead and sat up straighter, still holding her hand. "Okay ... We met up and it became a 'save Jorja' mission."

"I don't need saving. I don't want that many people involved. They have no fight in this."

I laughed. "I don't think you have a choice, and yes, they do. They care about you. You'd do the same for any of them."

"Are you going to school?" she asked, changing the subject.

"As soon as I leave here. I can't stay long. My dad told me to leave before visiting hours opened so your family didn't catch me here."

"Will you find a way to come back?"

"Rush and I will probably both be here tonight after visiting hours," I answered before looking at the clock on the wall. "I should go." I let go of her hand and stood.

"Toby, when I get out of here, can we go do something for fun that doesn't involve any of this mess?"

"I'd love that. Are you staying with your grandparents when you get out of here?"

"Unfortunately, but I'm sneaky. We'll figure out a way. They can't keep me caged up like some prisoner forever."

I smiled. "You tell me when and where, and I'm there."

"Is Rush coming by this morning, too?" She tucked some hair behind her ears.

"I don't know. I didn't ask. He was still asleep when I left."

"Is he still taking medicine to sleep?"

"He swore he isn't, but I'll make sure I check on him about it."

She smiled softly. "Thank you. I plan on talking to him, too."

I bent down and hugged her. "Get some rest. I'll see you later."

She held herself tightly to me a moment before releasing her grip and letting me go.

CHAPTER NINETEEN

Jorja

When the door opened, I hid the letter I was writing to Brian under my pillow. My plan was to ask a nurse to get it to him—since they were willing to sneak the boys in, it was worth a shot.

My grandfather—I mean, Jacob Bonovich—entered my room. I waited for his wife and my mother to trail in behind him, but when they didn't follow, the ache in the pit of my stomach grew. Not because I wanted to see them, but because a visit from Jacob alone couldn't be good.

He shut the door behind him and stood at the end of the bed.

I stared at him, allowing my eyes to form into a glare. "Yes?"

"They told me they will be letting you out tomorrow. They stated that you've been walking considerably well for someone with the amount of trauma you received to your hip. They say being young and athletic has helped."

I waited. That wasn't all he was here to say.

"With the new information regarding your biological father, the media has put their noses where they don't belong. Mr. Ellison has also decided to do an official paternity test and plans on fighting for parental rights."

I wondered if Edward Ellison knew he wasn't only fighting for parental rights, but he was starting a war.

I didn't respond. However, I kept my chin held high and never looked away. He needed to know I wasn't backing down, no matter how intimidating he was trying to be. I had already decided to be a good little girl and abide by his rules so I could snoop and find answers, but I wouldn't allow him to run all over me either. I had limits.

"No comment?" he prodded when I didn't respond.

I shook my head. "Why would I? It wouldn't change anything."

"I'm going to go meet with him. This is a very dangerous game he's playing. If your father, your rightful father, the one who raised you, were here, he'd end this quickly."

"You really didn't know this entire time that I wasn't Jerome's?" I found it so hard to believe. My mother told me they had no idea, but we were talking about Jacob Bonovich here. This man paid a lot of money to be several miles ahead of everyone else.

"I had suspicions, but it seems as though your father and mother are very good at keeping things a secret. What can I say? They did learn from the best." The way he adjusted his suit jacket when he said that reeked of confidence. No one should have this much power.

"What do you want from me, because we both know you aren't saying all of that just to inform me."

"Smart girl." He cleared his throat and set his dark eyes on mine. "I want you to tell the media that you want nothing to do with Edward Ellison nor his family. Tell them you are a Bonovich through and through and blood could never replace the bond and loyalty you have to this family. I have secured a lawyer who will be briefed on the narrative."

"And what do I get if I do it?"

His laugh could freeze an entire ocean. "Well, my dear, I allow you to live."

He just threatened my life. An ultimatum of following his rules or death. The way I wanted to respond would not get me the answers I needed, so I pushed back my anger and tried not to let it hurt.

"Yes, sir."

"Your first media appearance will be when they release you. If they ask about Edward Ellison, you tell them that he is not your father and that blood means nothing when he abandoned you."

But he didn't abandon me. His life and family were threatened. I nodded anyway.

He continued, "You tell them that you think he is the reason for the disappearance of your father. I want all allegations placed on him. Do you understand?"

Tears threatened to fall. This wasn't fair. They were going to ruin this man's life. I nodded again.

"And you should know ... I know those boys have been coming to see you. I've had a change of heart and decided to allow you to see them."

I waited for the reason and knew it would include his agenda.

"The saying is true, keep your enemies close. They are welcome in my home any time. All of your friends are. As a matter of fact, when you've healed a bit more, I say we throw a celebratory party in your honor." The way he showed all of his teeth in his smile unnerved me.

"What will that look like to the media? Throwing a party while your son is missing."

"We must celebrate with the people we love while we still have them here, don't you agree?" His laughter brought the room temperature down several degrees.

"Please don't hurt my friends."

"Do you plan on breaking our agreement?"

I shook my head.

"Then why on earth would you worry that I would hurt anyone?"

A single tear fell down my cheek, and I quickly wiped it away.

"While you may not be able to understand now, one day you will. Our love for you hasn't changed, Jorja. You are and will also be my granddaughter, blood or not. However, you are still a child, and children need to be taught lessons. Do you think everyone in the family has always just obeyed?"

"I assume not."

He chuckled. "Correct. As a matter of fact, as a child, I may have rebelled against the way of the Bonovich's. One day you will see all this life has to offer you. The power you can have."

He was wrong. Women in the family didn't have power. They were pretty little assets worn like an expensive wristwatch. They were pawns in a twisted game of Bonovich chess. The game had gone on long enough, and it would end with me.

"I'm tired," I said, hoping it'd make him leave.

"Get some rest. I'll see you later when your grandmother and mother come to see you."

I laid my head back and closed my eyes. When I heard the door open and shut, I opened my eyes again and reached under the pillow to get the letter I was writing to Brian. I finished writing it and smiled at the nurse when the door opened.

"You look like you're feeling better today," Amy, the nurse who had been on the day shift since I arrived, said.

"I'm feeling more like myself. It hurts, but I can manage."

She smiled softly as she took my vitals. "Do you need anything?"

"I need a favor." I held the folded letter in my hands. "Can you get this to my brother, Brian Bonovich? He's staying in the ICU, but I'm not allowed to see him."

She didn't take the letter. Instead, her face fell, and she looked at the ground before meeting my eyes. "No one told you?"

"No one told me what?"

"Jorja," her voice cracked, "I don't know how to tell you this, but your brother passed away earlier this morning. I figured that's why your grandfather was here this morning to see you first thing."

Crushing pain seared through my chest. She might as well have dug my heart out with her bare hands. Tears fell without warning at all. "What?" I barely got out.

"I shouldn't have been the one to tell you. I'm so sorry. I thought you already knew."

"How did he die?"

"Too much trauma I assume. I don't work on that floor, so I'm not sure exactly. I'm so sorry, Jorja." The nurse left without another word. What else could she say? She'd said enough.

I screamed.

I cried.

I begged for it to not be true.

In the pit of my stomach, I knew. I knew his death was on purpose. The way my grandfather smiled, the way he laughed ... He did it, or at least orchestrated it. He said we were turning the narrative around on Edward Ellison. They no longer needed the story about Brian to save Jerome's reputation. Or maybe it was a warning to me. To show me what would happen, that Jacob Bonovich would follow through on his word of killing me if I didn't obey.

Did he find out Olivia and Brian were working together? The man who shot me and I think shot Olivia ... Did he hear Olivia talking to me? We were talking so low that even if someone had been in the building, they couldn't have heard.

I was an idiot.

I should've known better. I killed the wrong man— if he was even dead. I saw Jerome the night I was shot. I know I did. Or maybe I was going crazy. Pain and shock can cause hallucinations.

I hugged one of the extra pillows and screamed into it.

This changed everything.

CHAPTER TWENTY

Rush

Who in their right mind sends out invitations to a funeral? Only those invited could attend Brian Bonovich's funeral, and I was shocked we were included. Jorja told us that her grandfather lifted the ban on seeing us, and while it all felt like a setup, it still meant we could see her and talk to her.

There was a dress code. All black, formal attire. Instead of the funeral being at the Bonovich funeral home, they were having it at Jorja's grandparents' estate.

Jorja got out of the hospital three days ago, and it'd been that long since I'd seen or spoken to her. Toby and I went to see her the night she found out her brother died, but she didn't feel like talking and asked us to leave. We found out later she turned all of her other friends away as well. She needed space, but it made me question how I was supposed to be around her when seeing her today.

After driving through the large gates, I was shocked at how long the road was before you ever arrived at the mansion. I knew her family was loaded, but never expected *this.* There was an entire staff of people: groundskeepers, butlers, and maids.

After Toby, Dad, and I got out of Dad's truck, a person took our keys with the promise to return them when we were ready. Toby laughed when the expensive looking man got into Dad's old dirty truck.

"Toto, I don't think we're in Kansas anymore," Toby said louder than he probably should have. I laughed anyway, but Dad gave us a warning glare.

A younger woman, dressed in a black dress and heels that she had to break her feet to get into, offered to show us the way, and we followed her inside.

Toby looked around as if he were memorizing every inch of this place. I kept my eyes straight ahead, like Dad, on the woman showing us the way. When we got to the room the woman called "The Gallery", I noticed the large space was full of artwork. They had Brian's open casket on display as if he were a piece of art as well. I found our group of friends sitting near the back, and after okaying it with Dad, Toby and I went to sit with them.

A priest spoke of scriptures and heaven and hell, but I kept looking at Jorja, who sat on the front row alongside her mother and grandparents. She was on the outer side of the row in a wheelchair. Despite all she had been through the past week, she still looked beautiful. Her hair was pulled up into a high ponytail with thin strands of curls placed perfectly around her face. She kept her eyes on her brother in the casket and had her right hand clenching a tissue.

The service came to an end, and after the viewing, they announced there would be no burial; it was Brian's request to be cremated. We were all ushered into a large dining hall where people walked around with platters full of food, drinks, and desserts. Dad mingled with everyone—being an officer in town, the type of people in attendance here were always trying to stay on his good side.

Tommy reached for a tall glass of wine as a server passed us and downed it before placing the empty glass on another tray of empty glasses as another server passed by. He was so quick about it, if you weren't watching you would've never noticed. I was worried about him. His dad was an alcoholic, and as much as he hated him for it, he was becoming just like him.

I laughed as Jena touched Toby's arm as she flirted. Toby kept backing away but could only go so far because of the crowd of people. Wren took notice and pulled Jena away, scolding her like a child. That made me laugh more.

Beck and Becca spoke quietly to one another, keeping their arms locked and scanning the room suspiciously. I looked to where their eyes were lingering and saw Jorja next to her mom as an older couple spoke to them. I could tell Jorja wasn't paying attention, her eyes distant and sad, but she nodded as they spoke anyway.

"Should we save her?" I asked Toby.

He dusted off his suit jacket where Jena's hands had been. "Save her? You could've saved me!"

I chuckled. "It looks like Wren handled it."

"For now," he mumbled. "And yes, let's go save her."

I looked at Tommy, Beck, and Becca. "We're going to see Jorja."

Tommy shook his head. "Correction. You're going to wait to see Jorja. You never interrupt conversations at these types of gatherings."

Why are they treating a funeral like a fancy dinner party?" Toby asked, clearly as disgruntled as I was.

"It's all show," Tommy answered with a shrug. "That's all these people want is a good show."

"But they were just trying to frame Brian. I'm surprised they gave him a funeral at all," I added.

Beck raised a brow. "As Tommy said, it's for show. Jorja made a scene on the news saying Brian was innocent. If they didn't throw him a funeral, it would've just caused more speculation. Now that Brian is dead, he can't be innocent or guilty. Just dead."

"So, what do we do in order to go talk to Jorja? Wait for a break in conversation?" Toby asked.

"Jorja knows how these things work. She will make her way to us when the time is right," Becca said with a comforting smile. "Just relax. You're making yourselves look desperate, and if you look too desperate, these people will use it to their advantage."

While we waited, we were approached by her grandfather. He shook our hands and smiled. "Jacob Bonovich. I'm so glad that you were able to come support Jorja during this tragic time." He nodded toward the rest of the group. "I believe we've all met before."

Everyone nodded, and he turned his attention back to Toby and me.

"I'm Rush," I said firmly.

"Toby," my brother said flatly.

"I insist you come visit more often. Jorja thinks the world of you two, and I'd like to get to know you both myself."

"I didn't know we were welcome here," Toby grumbled, and I eyed him nervously.

Toby put his hands into his pockets and kept his eyes on everything going on in the room rather than giving any more of his attention to Mr. Bonovich.

What was he doing? Being welcome there meant we could see Jorja.

I quickly started talking to ease the silence. "It was nice meeting you." I nudged Toby to make sure he would at least give him some acknowledgement.

"You both as well. I look forward to future meetings with you both."

I gave him a polite nod, and Toby went to give him the finger, but I quickly smacked his hand down.

"Let me have my fun," Toby said with a smirk as the man walked away.

"I've been trying, but you won't get the hint," Jena said, giggling.

Wren groaned. "Jena, stop it."

I laughed, but it faded quickly as I looked at my brother again. "I don't call that fun. You could be a bit more welcoming when around him so he doesn't ban us from Jorja again."

He rolled his eyes. "Yes, because I'm so welcoming."

"It doesn't matter. What matters is getting to see Jorja without all the barriers."

He scoffed. "He wants us around so he can watch us."

"Still welcome here when we weren't before."

He narrowed his eyes at me. "Welcome with a hidden agenda."

"That's why we play the game but better," Tommy said with a mischievous grin.

"War it is. I like war," Beck said as he pulled Becca closer to him.

Toby huffed. "That's it. I can't see her being miserable anymore." Before anyone could say anything, Toby started making his way through the crowd to Jorja.

CHAPTER TWENTY-ONE

Toby

I ignored my brother trailing behind me. I didn't care about stupid rich people's rules. Jorja was miserable, and following the rules for the sake of formality wasn't my thing.

I smiled kindly at the old couple boring her to death. "Mind if I steal Jorja for a bit?"

The woman held her wine glass to her lips and smiled. "Dashing. Jorja, who is this handsome young man?"

Rush was beside me then and spoke before I could. "Sorry if my brother is being rude. We can wait to speak with her."

"Two of them. How entertaining. I've always found twins fascinating. You know, there are rumors of twins in this family, but I have yet to meet any." The woman was clearly tipsy.

The man hushed his wife quickly. "Ignore her. She is always talking out of her head when she's been sipping wine. Have we met before? I don't recall seeing either of you at parties here before."

Rush spoke before I could. He held his hand out toward him. "No, sir. Rush and my brother, Tobias, True. We're close friends of Jorja's."

"I'm capable of speaking," I said quietly to Rush.

"Not gonna happen," Rush whispered back.

The man shook his hand. "Delighted to meet you. I'm Crismond Bonovich, Jorja's great uncle. And this lovely woman," he said, gesturing his head to his left, "is Missy Bonovich, my wife and her great aunt."

Crismond and Missy shook both of our hands, told Jorja and her mother bye with a hug, and left.

Jorja's mother forced a smile. "I'm not sure we've formally met. It's nice of you both to come to pay your respects."

"Mind if we steal Jorja for a bit?" Rush asked with a grin.

"It's not that hard, seeing anyone can wheel me away," Jorja said harshly. I knew being in a wheelchair was the last thing she wanted and was probably wearing on her mentally with everything else going on. When her eyes landed on me, she smiled a little.

"Not at all. Jorja, dear," her mother said, looking at her, "get some fresh air and show them the garden.

I'm sure they've had their fill of the stuffiness in here." She waved her hand around dramatically.

The entire group of friends caught wind of us going to the garden and they all followed. Once we made it, Jorja started taking off her heels.

"Umm, what are you doing?" Becca asked.

Jorja didn't answer but kept on until they were both off. She started getting out of the wheelchair, but I quickly stopped her by placing a hand on her shoulder.

"Whoa, what are you thinking?" I asked.

She looked up at me. "That I'm sick of looking weak in this damn chair." She moved my hand off her shoulder and slowly stood.

Rush and I were immediately and protectively on each side of her. She took both of our arms to steady herself. She was clearly in pain, but also not in the mood for any of us to point out this was a bad idea.

"Thank you all for coming," she said with a forced smile. "And before anyone asks, now, I'm not alright. I know without a doubt—" she stopped talking as a groundskeeper walked by and started again when he passed "—that my brother's death was on purpose. I don't have proof. Yet."

"We'll help," Becca said gently. "Just tell us what to do."

"I don't think any of you realize what getting involved with this family includes. We're talking about literal life or death situations."

"It doesn't matter," Tommy stated firmly. "We stick together, no matter what. I'm sick of rich people getting their way. And I speak for everyone when I say we are sick of the hold the Bonovich name has on this town. It's time we change the narrative."

Jorja's eyes shifted to everyone before speaking. "Then we need to have a serious conversation." She looked at Rush and then at me. I knew what that meant. She wanted to tell them everything.

"When?" I asked her.

She looked around before carefully sitting back down into the wheelchair. "Everyone lean in close because I'm only going to say this once."

Everyone leaned in, but I already knew what she was going to say.

"I killed Jerome Bonovich." No mention of mine and Rush's involvement. I figured she wanted to keep it that way.

Everyone stood up straight again and no one uttered a word.

She let it sink in a bit before she started talking again. "But I saw him. I know I did. The night I was shot. My sister was there, too." She spoke quietly, but loud enough for us to hear.

Maybe that's why her mother suggested we go to the garden. Did her mother know, too? There was one way to find out.

"Who all knows besides us?" Beck asked her.

She shook her head. "No one."

"Did your sister try to hurt you?" Becca asked.

She shook her head again. "No. She was there, wanting to help me. I think she may have been shot, too. I haven't seen her since."

"Oh my god," Wren breathed out. "This is crazy. Why do you think you saw *him*?"

"I don't know, but I have suspicions after hearing a conversation a moment ago." Jorja looked at me and Rush. "My great uncle was quick to interrupt my great aunt about there being twins in this family. What if Jerome was a twin?"

"Wouldn't you have known, though?" Wren asked.

Jena still hadn't said a word. She looked like she was in shock.

The thought of Jerome being a twin hit me when I remembered something I had tried to forget. Something I would never tell anyone. I looked at Jorja, almost opening my mouth, but closed it quickly before I could say a word—pushing it to the back of my mind where it would stay forever.

Jorja shrugged. "What I've learned is that family secrets have a way of staying hidden until they're ready to reveal themselves. Especially in this family. Nothing surprises me anymore. But," she continued after a dramatic sigh, "I could be wrong."

"It's a risk for sure, but I'm intrigued," Tommy said with a playful grin. "And who doesn't love a good mystery to solve?"

I laughed. "So, about that Mystery Van ..."

CHAPTER TWENTY-TWO

Jorja

Three weeks ago, I was almost killed.

Three weeks ago, I saw my sister before she disappeared again.

Three weeks ago, my brother died.

Three weeks ago, I told my entire friend group I killed Jerome Bonovich.

And three weeks ago, I also thought I saw Jerome alive.

The idea that he was possibly a twin wouldn't let me sleep. The idea that he was possibly a twin also pushed me to work even harder in physical therapy so I could find out for myself. Physical limitations made the pursuit of the truth impossible. But today, I was finally able to walk on my own. I recovered faster than normal patients according to my doctor. Being young, in shape, and *very* determined got me here, but unfortunately, cheer was out indefinitely because of the surgery and level of trauma to my hip. That was the least of my worries, though.

The biggest question that haunted me the most was, if Jerome was a twin, did I kill the right one? The quest to find answers took a turn I would've never expected.

The man I killed looked and acted like Jerome the night I poisoned the drink. Nothing would've ever told me otherwise had my great aunt not said what she said. Not to mention how hasty my great uncle was to silence her and change the subject. There had to be records in this house somewhere if it were true, and if my suspicions were correct, this was a secret Jacob and Henrietta kept from the entire family.

I looked at my phone when it started ringing and saw Toby's name flash across the screen. I finally got my phone back, but not the keys to my car. I was allowed to go to school and back to the estate. I could have friends come here, but not go out with them. I was being watched, there was no doubt about that, but it just meant I had to be smarter about how I did things.

"Hey," I said as I answered with a huge smile.

"Hey, did you finish your homework?"

"Yup!" I heard a car door shut. "What are you doing?"

"About to knock on your grandparents' front door."

"You're here?" I squealed.

"I am. Just handing my keys off to the valet. I'll never get used to that, by the way."

I laughed. "Be right there!"

I couldn't move as fast as I'd like, but I made my way as quickly as I could downstairs and saw Toby was already let inside. A maid was taking his jacket when his eyes landed on me. A smile spread across his face as he made his way over to me. When his arms found their way around me, I melted against him and hugged him tightly.

We both looked at the door when there was a knock and pulled apart so I could answer it.

Rush immediately hugged me, and I felt his body tense.

"You didn't tell me you were coming," he said to Toby, tightening his hold on me.

"Was I supposed to?" Toby asked with a chuckle, but I could tell he didn't find anything funny at all.

Rush loosened his hold on me so he could look me over. "How are you feeling? Better?"

The tension was so thick it was hard to smile, but I managed to anyway. "Same as when you asked me a thousand times today." I laughed.

I added distance between me and both the boys. "Come with me. I want to show you both something."

Toby walked on my left while Rush walked to my right. I hated the obvious friction between the two but was thankful they both came over. I needed to say something to drown out the awkward silence.

"They stopped the search for Jerome," I said, walking a little ahead of them so they could follow me as I started up the stairs. "However, the family has people on the inside looking." I knew I could talk about all of this right now, because the security cameras couldn't pick up what was being said on the stairs. I learned that by seeing the maids whispering on them. The observatory where we were headed was also a safe place to talk—no cameras at all.

"Is your grandfather home?" Rush asked.

"Jacob is away on a business trip," I stated flatly. "And his wife is out with her rich girlfriends having dinner." I felt Toby's hand on my lower back as I started to struggle with the stairs. I looked at him and smiled. "I'm fine. Just a little slower than normal."

Before I could object, Rush was lifting me into his arms and carrying me up the stairs. "Just tell me which way."

I met his eyes and playfully patted his chest. "Put me down. I can't get stronger if I don't walk by myself."

He was hesitant but followed my request.

"The doctor released me to walk fully on my own and rest as needed. I promise I'm fine," I said when I noticed their looks of concern.

Once we made it to the top of the stairs, I took the hallway to the left, the one opposite my room. "This place is full of history and secrets. I know I promised all of you I wouldn't start snooping alone, but I couldn't help myself. Where I'm taking you, I found by accident, but it's my favorite. It's crazy ... I grew up coming to this house every single Sunday but never once knew this room existed. There were certain parts of the house that were off limits, but since Jacob is out of town, I took advantage of the freedom to roam."

We entered a door that led to a spiral staircase. I knew I'd be extra sore after this, but it'd be worth it to show them.

"This place has a lot of stairs," Toby said through laughter.

"How far up?" Rush asked.

"Just don't think about how far and keep following me. It'll be worth it. I promise."

I kept a slow but steady pace, ignoring the throbbing pain in my hip and leg. "I always thought the gold domes on the top of the house were for looks, but it appears," I said as we reached the top and entered the circular room, "they were observatories."

"Like NASA?" Toby asked.

I nodded as I laughed. "But on a smaller scale."

I stopped in the center of the room near the large telescope and let the guys take in the full room window and ceiling. From the outside of the home, you could see the two gold dome shapes on each side of the house that you couldn't see in. In here, it was a full view of the sky and property below. The windows were so surprisingly clear that if felt like if you kept walking, you'd walk right off the edge of the floor.

"Isn't it amazing?" I asked, turning in a full circle to take it all in myself.

Toby walked over to the large telescope that stood in the center of the room with me. "Wow," he said as he ran his fingers over it.

"I have no idea how to work it, but I bet it's awesome." I pointed to the large table on the right side of the room that had books about stars. "There's a ton of information over there. I never knew Jacob and Henrietta were into space like this."

"Or maybe it was Jerome. He was raised in this house, right?"

My eyes widened, and I grinned. "Toby! You're brilliant!"

Rush had been staring in the distance when my loud voice caught his attention. He looked at me. "Why is my brother brilliant?" He started walking over.

"I have no idea what I said to make her think that," Toby said, chuckling.

"I've been so consumed by the idea of Jerome being a twin that I didn't even think about the fact that he and possibly his brother were raised here! Their rooms ... They'd have rooms here."

"You've had a lot going on, I'm sure you would've thought of it sooner or later." Toby put his hands into his jean pockets. "I don't know how you can think of anything at all. I've been worried about you."

I smiled softly. "I'm fine."

"Liar," Rush said through a grunt.

I shrugged. "It's all just becoming the norm now. I don't know any different."

"You lost your brother, Jorja. None of this is normal, and it's okay to not be okay." Rush stating the obvious made me angry.

The smile I had forced faded quickly. "I'm envious of my brother."

"But he's—" Rush started, but I cut him off.

"Dead."

Rush nodded, and Toby remained silent, staring at the telescope.

"Exactly. He's dead, but he's not here dealing with all of this. It's over for him. He's free. So, yes, I'm envious of him."

Toby's eyes scrunched together as he looked at me.

I shook my head and met his eyes. "Don't worry. I'm not thinking about harming myself, but," I continued, looking at Rush, "if you were me, you'd be envious of him, too."

"It's really beautiful here," Toby said as he looked at the sun starting to set. He'd never know how much I appreciated him changing the subject. "Are we being watched here?"

I shook my head. The way the orange glow from the setting sun illuminated Toby's face made my heart flip in my chest. Toby's eyes met mine, and, for a moment, we just stared at one another. I had almost forgotten Rush was in the room, but he made it known when he cleared his throat and moved the telescope.

"Let's figure out how this thing works so we can see the stars," he said, his eyes narrowing on Toby.

Toby's cheeks reddened, and he chuckled, looking at the floor. Whatever happened between us just then was more than obvious, even if I couldn't quite describe exactly what it was.

I went to the large table of books and found a user manual for the telescope. I started flipping through it as I walked over to the guys standing at the telescope. Toby moved it until it pointed more north. I watched as he leaned over to look in it and he smiled, signifying he found something.

"Did you figure it out?" I asked.

"It's blurry."

Rush stood close and peered over my shoulder as I searched the table of contents for focusing help.

"Everything okay between us?" Rush asked quietly as I flipped pages.

I stopped turning pages and looked up at him. "Why wouldn't it be?"

He shrugged and looked at his brother. I knew what he was saying without even saying it, but I didn't know what to tell him. Anything I said wouldn't be what he wanted to hear, and I wasn't having this conversation right now. I just wanted to enjoy this night with them, not thinking about all the issues that'd be waiting on me as soon as they left, and I was faced with another sleepless night of reality.

I looked at the book again and finished turning to the correct page. I walked over to Toby and started explaining what to do. I could feel Rush watching, so I was careful with how I interacted with Toby.

"I think I got it!" Toby said excitedly. He placed his hand on my lower back and guided me to the scope so I could look.

I bent down, Toby's hand still on my back, as I looked through. "What am I looking for?"

"I don't know, but you can see the stars more clearly."

I laughed and smiled as I looked at the stars. They were just a tad brighter and bigger than looking at them with the naked eye.

"This book explains how to find Jupiter," Rush said, and Toby and I both looked at him. He had a book he didn't have a moment ago, carefully reading. "It says to first look toward the southeastern to southwestern part of the sky. Jupiter should be one of the brightest objects up there, appearing as a steady, bright light—brighter than most stars."

I took a step to the side to let Toby try to look for it.

"What's next?" Toby asked as he adjusted the direction of the telescope.

Rush moved his finger along the page as he read. "Once you've found the bright light, point the telescope toward it. Use the finder scope to center Jupiter in your field of view. Then, look through the main eyepiece and adjust the focus knob until the image is clear. The book says with the telescope properly focused, you should see some of Jupiter's cloud bands and maybe even its Galilean moons around it."

"I found it!" Toby said excitedly. He grabbed my hand, guiding me gently to the telescope and instructed me on what to do.

When I spotted it, I grinned. My eyes were immediately drawn to the bands around it. The dark and light strips wound around the surface that looked like a giant marble with swirls of brown and reds. "It's beautiful." I took a step back and reached for the book Rush had. "Look at it!"

He handed me the book and looked into the telescope. A smile spread across his face.

Finding Jupiter ignited a fire that turned into countless hours of us researching and finding as many planets and constellations as we could.

After walking the guys out and telling them bye, I went out to the garden where I could clear my head. It was the only place I could feel Brian and Olivia because we had spent so much time playing hide and seek in the maze of plants when we were kids. I looked up at the sky, amazed at how differently it looked from down here than through the telescope in the observatory. You couldn't tell me God wasn't real with the way the universe worked in perfect harmony.

I had just started thinking about where to start looking for Jerome and his possible twin's bedrooms when I heard footsteps from behind me. I jerked my body around, hissing from the pain in my side from the forceful movement.

"It's me," Toby whispered as he came into view in the moonlight.

"I thought you left." I rubbed my side.

"I did, and then ..." He looked at my side. "Are you okay?"

I stopped rubbing my side. "Yeah. Toby, what are you doing back here?"

His forehead creased as he frowned. "I don't know. I was leaving and the craziest thing happened ... My hands stopped listening to my brain and turned the truck around and ended up right back here."

"Your hands?" I raised a brow and couldn't help the smile that spread across my face.

He nodded and looked at me as seriously as he could. "Damn things won't listen."

The distance started slowly closing between us.

"And where's Rush?"

"On his way home."

There was barely any distance between us now. "And what will he think about you coming back here?"

He brushed hair out of my face and tucked it gently behind my ear. "These damn hands just won't listen ..."

My hands weren't listening either. I put my arms around his neck with no logical explanation of why I was allowing this or why I wanted this.

"These damn lips," he barely uttered in a whisper.

Before I could register what we were doing, his mouth pressed against mine. The warmth from his lips spread through every inch of my body, igniting a fire I didn't even know existed.

Did I kiss him first?

Or did he kiss me?

It didn't matter. It happened either way.

When the kiss ended, tears filled my eyes. "Don't fall for me, Toby."

He wiped my tears away with his thumb and whispered, "I'm afraid it's too late."

CHAPTER TWENTY-THREE

Rush

I knew exactly where my brother was. I saw from my rearview mirror when he whipped his truck into a U-turn and hightailed it back to Jorja. So, there I was, sitting on my tailgate waiting.

I told him it was okay, but it didn't *feel* okay. I wanted what was best for Jorja, but I couldn't help the selfish urge to claim territory and say she was mine. I couldn't decide that; she'd have to decide that, and I had to figure out how to not be a total dick about it all. But right then, in the moment, it hurt so much it felt like I couldn't breathe.

Maybe she'd tell him she didn't feel that way for him.

Maybe she'd tell him what she tells me ... That she isn't ready to be in a relationship with everything going on.

Maybe ...

My rational thoughts vanished and turned into rage when I saw his headlights and truck come into view. As soon as he parked and got out, I saw his disheveled hair and my thoughts sharpened into one single focus. I squared my shoulders with clenched fists at my sides.

"What the hell, Toby?"

He walked past me, ignoring me, but I caught up to him in the front yard. I grabbed his shoulder, and he shrugged me off then turned to face me. His smirk only fueled my anger. Without another word, I launched myself at him, my fist aiming straight for his jaw. He dodged, his fist aiming for my face, but I blocked it with my arm, feeling the jolt of the impact spread up my shoulder. I swung again, connecting my fist to his cheekbone.

A red flush spread across his face as he staggered back. Rage filled his eyes as a round of several punches made connections to my gut and face. Each blow drove me back a step, but I refused to back down. With a grunt, I lunged forward, my fist colliding with his left eye. I felt blood trickling down my chin from my lip and wiped it on my sleeve and we circled each other like fighters in a caged ring. The sounds of fists against flesh and bone drowned out any thoughts of stopping.

Resentment and bitterness regarding Jorja fueled every punch. There were no signs of stopping, until I spotted Dad sitting on the steps of the front porch watching us. Toby noticed where I was looking and took a step back from me. As the adrenaline slowly faded, I looked at my brother, his chest rising and falling with each breath. There was a flicker of something in his eyes—regret, maybe, I wasn't sure.

"It was only a matter of time before this happened," Dad said as he stood. He was still in uniform.

Blood dripped from both mine and Toby's split lips and swollen eyes, but I knew neither of us would admit we were in pain. I looked away from both Toby and Dad.

"Was anything resolved?" Dad asked, crossing his arms over his chest.

Neither of us answered.

"You're not going in the house until it's resolved. You're going to sit out here and fight until you tire or come to a resolution."

I didn't have it in me to fight anymore. Not physically. I looked at Toby, waiting for him to say what he wanted to do.

He refused to look at me. He looked at Dad instead. "Can I go for a drive and clear my head?"

"If you choose to do that, Rush will sit outside and wait for you to come back. I mean it, I don't give a damn if you have to sleep in your trucks. You won't come back into this house until you fix your relationship. One day, all you two will have is each other. I won't allow my boys to ruin their relationship over a girl."

"Yes, sir," Toby answered before going to his truck and leaving.

Dad raised a brow at me. "Who started it?"

I didn't want to answer. I rubbed the tension in my neck. "Me."

"Why?"

I sighed heavily. "We went to Jorja's, and after we both left, he went back."

"And?"

I shrugged.

"That's not an answer, Rush."

I sighed heavily again and looked at him. "I don't know if anything happened."

"You assumed?"

I nodded. "Yes, sir."

"And if something did happen, why are you mad? You're not dating Jorja, unless something changed that I don't know about."

I looked at him, mentally preparing myself for him to take Toby's side like he always does. "We aren't dating, and I told Toby it was okay if he pursued things with Jorja because I want her happy. When I saw him, I snapped. He didn't tell me he was going back, but he did."

"Does he have to tell you he's going back? And, Rush, you can't give someone permission with something like this. You say you want Jorja happy, but don't you also want to see your brother happy?"

"Yes ..." I clenched my jaw tight. "Just not with the girl I love."

He laughed quietly. "I'm not questioning your feelings about Jorja, but I do want you to consider the idea that a future with her is unlikely. Both of you need to consider that before you go ruining your relationship with the person who will have your back for life. You both have this 'I can save her' hero complex going on. I don't want you two involved with her or that family at all, but I also know you both won't care what I say and do it anyway no matter the consequences. I'm choosing my battles in this fight, and you both need to do the same. There is no future with a girl like her, Rush. If she makes it out of this thing alive, she'll run like hell from this place. Trust me, I know."

I thought about Mom and him. "It's different with Jorja. She isn't addicted to drugs."

"Different situation, same concept. You don't know everything about why your mom and I didn't work out. There is a reason you don't know a thing about her parents and they've never been involved in you or your brother's life."

Toby and I never had grandparents or aunts or uncles involved in our lives. Dad's parents died before we could ever meet them, and he was an only child. Mom's family disowned her, and that's all I knew.

"Tell me then."

He shook his head and his eyes filled with sadness. "Not right now. Just know I get it. I lost my best friend because we loved the same girl."

Dad never talked to us about his past life with us, but I wished he would. "I won't give up on Jorja, Dad."

He nodded. "Because you're too much like me, and so is your brother. You both are going to have to let Jorja decide what she wants and learn to be okay with it."

"If one of us does end up with her, will you support it?"

He smiled softly. "Son, I will always support the both of you, and I hope you prove me wrong with how I predict things will end."

I looked at the street in front of our house. "Do I really have to wait to get cleaned up until he comes back?"

He laughed. "Yup. I'm going in. When you two fix it, let me know." He went inside, and I heard him lock the door. I had a house key, but I didn't want to find out what would happen if I snuck in, so I sat on the porch and waited for Toby to return.

CHAPTER TWENTY-FOUR

Toby

I stared at Mom's grave as I stood over it.

It was the first time I had been out there since we'd buried her. I wasn't really sure what motivated me to go out there now, all bloody and bruised. Her and I never saw eye-to-eye. I mean, what mother would be okay with taking one child and not the other? Dad never told me everything about them, but I do know she was the one who chose to leave. Dad didn't want to fight with her or deal with the court, so he just agreed when she took Rush and left me with him. When we were little, Rush and I would go back and forth between houses during breaks. As we got older and she was consumed by drugs, I stopped going and Rush would come here instead. All her and I did was argue.

"My bright beautiful boys," she'd say in her drug-induced state of mind, *"I love you so much. I'd do anything for you."*

It was a lie.

She loved her drugs more.

Rush believed she quit, and I never did.

"How's your beautiful boy looking now, Mom?" I kicked a rock at her headstone. I wiped the stupid tears that fell. I didn't cry for her, just what could've been. She could've been a good mom.

How ironic she was buried in the graveyard owned by the man who pulled the trigger. She wasn't even safe from drugs where she was laid to rest; Jorja said they used this place for transport. That's when I remembered the tunnels she spoke of. I looked at the door to the storage building she said she believed led to underground tunnels. I looked over my shoulder before heading over to it, and then I tugged on the door a few times.

"I wouldn't do that," I heard a female's hushed voice say from behind me.

My body tensed as I turned to see who it was.

"Sorry, not Jorja." She laughed. "I'm Olivia. Her sister."

I knew who she was. Everyone in Grove did. She looked older, slightly different, but still her.

"You're alive?"

She laughed and held her hands out at her sides. "Unless I'm a ghost. Do you believe in ghosts?"

"Jorja said you were shot."

"I was. I healed. How is she?"

Anger filled me. "You left her there that night!"

"I had to. I didn't have a choice. It'd ruin everything." She looked around before meeting my eyes. "Look, we can't keep standing out here. What are you doing here looking like ... that?" She motioned to my face.

"Long story. What are you doing here?" I asked, avoiding answering her question.

"Meeting someone. You should—" She stopped talking when we heard footsteps. "Dammit. Looks like you're staying."

I tensed when I saw Peter walking over.

"What's he doing here?" he snapped as he looked at me. "Rush—" He stopped talking as he got a better look at me. "Tobias? What happened to your face?"

"Oh, shit, you're not Rush?" Olivia said in shock.

"What's going on here?" I asked in a snap.

Peter and Olivia looked at each other.

"He cares about Jorja. He can help us," Peter said.

Olivia stared at him, narrowing her eyes a bit. "Can we trust him, though?"

Peter nodded.

"Trust me for what?"

"We can't talk about it here. Come on," Olivia said, motioning for us to follow.

I didn't budge, causing both Peter and her to look at me like I had lost my mind.

"I don't know what I'm following you both into." It didn't help that I still wanted to beat the hell out of Peter for what he put Jorja through and was pissed Olivia left Jorja the night she was shot.

"Jorja is my sister. I have tons of dirt on her so-called-family. We're taking them down and getting her out of there," Peter said firmly. "My dad isn't going to stop fighting for custody of her. We all know they made Jorja say she doesn't want anything to do with him. We know everything, and we're fighting back."

"Jorja is making plans to fight back," I said.

Olivia shook her head adamantly. "There is no way in hell she can do that. Not alone."

"She's not alone," I said.

Olivia walked closer to me. "You tell her to stop. She'll end up dead like Brian. All of you will. I've been studying this family for years. I know what I'm doing. Tell her to let me handle this and wait for a signal."

"A signal?"

She nodded. "She'll know. Peter will make contact with her. Tell her to stop, Tobias. You have to. Things have gone too far. They killed Brian. They'll kill her next without even batting an eye. Tell her to stop," she repeated, urging me with tears in her eyes.

I nodded. "Okay. I'll tell her." I looked at Peter. "You hurt Jorja again, and I'll kill you."

Olivia grinned as she looked at Peter. "I like him."

"Oh, yes, he's such a joy to be around," Peter mumbled, but he also laughed a little. "You never answered about what happened. You look like you've been run over," he said, looking at me with a disgusted face.

"I don't want to talk about it. You two go do whatever it is you're doing, and I'll go tell Jorja."

Olivia smiled softly. "Thank you, Tobias. I will go to her when the time is right."

It felt weird trusting her when I didn't even know her, but my gut told me she meant it.

CHAPTER TWENTY-FIVE

Jorja

I was slowly making my way around the left wing of the house. It was where all the guest bedrooms were, so I figured it had to be where Jerome and his possible twin's rooms were. There were eight doors, and just as I was about to open the first door on the right, my phone started ringing. I saw Toby's name and answered it.

"Hey," I whispered.

"Why are you whispering?"

"I don't know," I said in a normal tone with a small laugh.

"I need you to listen to me. Stop looking for answers, okay?"

I scrunched my nose. "What? Why?"

"I don't want to say on the phone."

I took my hand off the doorknob. "Toby, what's going on?"

He sighed. "Just stop, okay?"

My chest felt heavy. "Is everything okay?"

"Yes and no."

"Where are you?" I could feel myself starting to panic. Something wasn't right.

"In my truck at the graveyard."

My hands began to tremble. "Why? Toby, what the hell are you doing there?"

"Seeing my mom."

"But the graveyard isn't safe at night," I almost shouted.

"I'm aware, but I needed to get away from the house."

I frowned. "Why?"

"I don't want to talk about it."

"But—"

"What are you doing?" Jacob snapped. He wasn't supposed to be home yet.

"Jorja, who is that?" Toby asked.

I hung up on Toby and put the phone in my back pocket. "I was on the phone with my friend just walking around the place. I've never seen it all before and wanted to explore."

He scowled down at me. "You didn't have permission."

"I didn't know I needed it." I kept my eyes on his. I could feel my phone in my back pocket vibrating over and over again and knew it was Toby trying to call back. I was sure he was panicking, but I couldn't answer him right then.

"If someone doesn't say you can roam, then you must assume that roaming isn't allowed."

"I'm sorry. I didn't know I had to ask. I will from now on. So, I thought you wouldn't be home yet. Everything go okay on your business trip?" I asked, hoping he'd go with changing the subject rather than scolding me more.

I noticed the glass of shallow brown liquid which brought my mind to the night I killed who I *hoped* was Jerome. He took a sip and shrugged slightly. "Things moved along quicker than anticipated."

I nodded, but wanted to ask what he was doing down this wing. Did he come to think? Or maybe to remember raising his child or children? Maybe he came to hide more skeletons in the numerous closets. Either way, it was apparent he didn't want me there which led me to believe I was exactly where I needed to be for answers.

"Go get some rest. You have to be up early."

When I started to speak, he interrupted me.

"Earlier than normal. You're switching schools."

"What?" My body tensed. "Did my mother approve this?"

He nodded. "You'll be going to the private school in Villa."

"Villa Preparatory? That's an hour away."

He laughed coolly. "And I have a very capable driver. One of the maids has already laid your uniform out in your room. If I had it my way, you would've started there in kindergarten. You are above the disgrace that is public school."

Tears burned my eyes. "When was this decided?"

"Today." He motioned for me to start walking.

"Why?" I asked, hopeful he would answer, but he didn't. Instead, he urged me to keep moving.

My phone continued to vibrate in my back pocket as I walked, and Jacob trailed behind me. As soon as it stopped, it would start back up again. As long as he was in sight, I couldn't answer it. I picked up my pace to get to my room as quickly as possible. What did Toby know that I didn't? It was odd how just as Toby was telling me to back off the search for answers, Jacob showed up.

When I made it to my room, I shut the door and locked it behind me. I called Toby back, but he didn't answer. I looked at the uniform on the bed and huffed. It was exactly what I expected because I had seen people on social media from that school. Some of them followed me on Instagram. Navy blazer, white button down, tall white socks, and a navy pencil skirt with a small slit in the back. I looked to the floor and saw the black heels.

Just as I was putting the uniform into my closet, I heard knocking on the glass doors that led to the balcony. I stepped out of the closet and my heart raced when I saw Toby standing there. I let him in quickly and before I could comment on the cut under his eye, the bruising, and the busted lip, he wrapped me in his arms.

"What are you doing here? How'd you get in?"

"I had to see if you were okay. I panicked when you hung up. I climbed the tree." He pulled back to look at me.

"Did you get hurt climbing up here?" I gently touched the side of his face. I looked at his bloody shirt that also was full of grass stains.

"I didn't get hurt coming up here."

"Did someone hurt you at the graveyard?"

He shook his head. "No one hurt me at the graveyard."

I frowned deeply. "Then what happened?"

"I had a fight with Rush."

"Why?"

He shook his head. "That's not important right now. Now that I'm here, I need to tell you why I needed you to stop the search for answers."

I had so many things, questions, swirling through my head. Where did he park? Did he run through the surrounding woods to get here?

"Are you listening?" he asked.

I looked up at him and nodded, still going through all the questions in my mind. Why did him and Rush get into a fight?

"While I was at the graveyard, I saw Olivia and Peter."

He had my full attention now. "What?"

"They have a plan and told me to tell you to stop or you'll end up dead."

My brow furrowed. "My sister is okay?"

He nodded, and relief filled me.

"Peter was with her? Why?"

"Yes. I don't know any details, but I trust them, Jorja. I will tell everyone else, but the search stops for now. Okay?"

"But—"

"The search stops," he demanded, with such urgency I could feel his body trembling.

I put my head to his chest and hugged him tightly. "Okay," I whispered. "I will stop." When I felt his body relax, I looked up at him. "Tell me about the fight with Rush."

"It's because I was with you instead of going home when he did."

I took a step back and wrapped my arms around myself. "Who started it?"

"He did."

Anger filled me. "He hit you first?"

Toby nodded. "We'll work it out, Jorja. Don't worry about it."

"But he had no right."

Toby scoffed. "Maybe not, but he also cares for you and wants to be with you. That's no secret."

"But we're not together. You two shouldn't be fighting over me. This—"

"Don't worry about it," he said, cutting me off. "We'll work it out. This is between me and him."

I chewed on the inside of my cheek to keep from saying more. I didn't want anyone fighting over me, but if they were, it was my fault. I allowed Toby to kiss me. I gave Rush hope for us. Choosing to drop the subject for a moment, I looked at Toby and told him about Villa Prep. "I won't be at Grove High anymore starting tomorrow."

His eyes widened. "What do you mean?"

I shrugged, too mentally exhausted to answer. "I'm scared, Toby. Everything is so out of hand. I feel like I'm grasping at air with no way to hold onto anything. I just want to run away. I want nothing more than for this family to burn and watch it happen, but I'm tired. I just want to get away." I touched just above his bruising eye. "Everything I touch I ruin. Your fight with Rush is my fault."

He shook his head. "That's not true."

I smiled sadly. "Look at you and Rush. My brother is dead because I pushed for answers. I killed a man who may or may not have been Jerome. Everything is falling apart, and I can't win this. Peter and Olivia can't win this. The Bonoviches will always stay a step ahead. They probably know you're in here with me now. Everything and everyone who is around me could get hurt or potentially die."

A sureness filled Toby's eyes. "I won't give up on you, so whatever it is that you're implying right now, I won't allow it. I'm here through it all."

"Until you're not here because you've been killed. The best thing you and Rush can do is forget about me, Toby. Live a normal life. Be safe and happy."

His eyes narrowed, and he shook his head. "No."

I took several steps away from him. "Yes. I'm not giving you an option. This is my decision. I'm doing this all alone now. Tell everyone. I give up. I surrender. I will just comply and be the good little girl they want me to be. I can't let anyone else die because of this!"

He took a step toward me, making me take another step back.

"Leave," I demanded. I began to sob. "Go home, Toby. Don't ever come back."

"No," he said, taking several more steps toward me.

I kept walking backward until my back was against the wall, and then there was no space between us. He lifted my chin gently and kissed me quickly, then he put his forehead to mine. "I'm not going to run away like a coward when things get hard. I'm in this with you whether you want me to be or not. I'm choosing this. I'm choosing you. I don't care what happens to me."

"I can't lose you," I cried. "I care what happens to you."

"You won't lose me."

I shook my head as he wiped my tears away. "You don't know that."

We both looked at the door when there was a knock. "Jorja," I heard Henrietta say. "What's going on in there? I heard yelling."

My eyes widened, and I grabbed Toby's arm, leading him to the closet. I shoved him inside before shutting the door. I went to the bedroom door and opened it.

"I was just talking to my friend on the phone. I'm upset that I'm being forced to go to Villa Prep." I wiped my cheeks. "I graduate this year, Grandmother. I've been at my school since kindergarten. Please don't make me do this."

She came into my room and shut the door behind her. "Jorja, I'm in your room right now," she said, lowering her voice, "because the maids were whispering about a boy being here. You tell him to leave. You go to Villa and find answers to save this family."

My mouth fell open. "W-what?"

"I'm on your side, Jorja. I need to go before your grandfather comes looking for me." She hugged me and quickly left the room.

In a matter of seconds, I learned two things:

There were answers at Villa Preparatory School about the secrets of this family.

My grandmother was really on my side.

"Shit," I mumbled, remembering Toby was still in my closet. I hurried to the closet to let him out.

CHAPTER TWENTY-SIX

Rush

This was ridiculous. Toby was still gone, and it was going on midnight. I knew he didn't want to go to school looking like this, in the same clothes, just as much as I didn't want to. Dad was standing on business and refused to let me inside. He wouldn't even toss me out a pillow or blanket. I text Jorja while I waited miserably inside my truck.

Me: Are you up?

Jorja: Yeah, and Toby just left here. He told me about the fight.

Of course he went there, and I was mad at myself for not thinking of going there myself.

Me: What's going on, Jorja?

Jorja: With what exactly? There's a lot going on.

Me: I thought we were something, or at least becoming something. Just tell me straight up what's going on between you and my brother.

Jorja: I don't know. I'm really confused right now, Rush. I didn't mean to get caught up with feelings for both of you. I'm in a really weird headspace right now, and a relationship is the last thing I need or want.

Me: So you and him aren't dating?

Jorja: No.

Me: But you have feelings for him?

Jorja: Yes.

Me: And feelings for me?

Jorja: Yes.

I wanted to be angry with her.

I wanted to be angry with Toby.

But how could I be mad at either of them? Feelings aren't something you can help, they just ... happen. I reacted poorly tonight. I knew throwing the first punch was wrong. Demanding answers from Jorja with her in such a vulnerable time as this was wrong. Forcing myself to send the next text was hard, but I did it anyway.

Me: I understand and I'm not going anywhere. I'm your friend forever despite what happens, okay?

And I meant it, even if my stubbornness and urge to be the brother that won tried to take over.

Jorja: Thank you, Rush. Now work things out with Toby.

Me: I will.

Jorja: Good. You should also know that I'm no longer going to school at Grove High. I'll be transferring to Villa Preparatory in the morning.

My heart sank.

Me: Why?

Jorja: Because apparently I'm above public education.

Me: When can I see you again?

Jorja: Tomorrow after school? I should be back here around 5:00.

Me: I'll be there.

Jorja: See you then :)

I looked up from my phone when Toby pulled in beside me. I had to remind myself I was being an asshole and had to fix this as I got out of the truck and walked over to him. He put his hands into his pockets and stared at me.

"I'm sorry," I said calmly. "I was wrong for doing what I did."

"Do you mean that, or do you just want to go inside and take a shower?"

I maintained eye contact with him and looked at him seriously. "I mean it, Toby. I'm sorry. I was wrong about everything."

"I'm way past hiding my feelings for her to save yours, Rush. Are you sure you can be okay with that if she chooses me?"

I nodded, even though my chest filled with a heaviness that made it hard to breathe. "I have to be okay with it. And if she chooses me, can you live with that?"

He nodded. "Yes."

Toby hugged me first, and I hugged him back. We stayed in an embrace for a few seconds before pulling apart. I looked at him and then down at myself.

"We need to get cleaned up."

He laughed. "Yeah ... Jorja isn't going to our school anymore."

I nodded. "Yeah, she told me in a text."

"Something shocking happened while I was there. I was hiding in her closet because her grandmother, I mean, Henrietta, came in. She told Jorja she was on her side and to find answers at the private school. She said to save the family."

My eyes widened. "Are you serious?"

He rubbed the back of his neck. "Yeah, and while I was out, I first went to the graveyard to see Mom. While there, Peter and Olivia showed up. They told me they were working to help Jorja and to tell her to stop searching. I went to Jorja to tell her to stop the search, and she was going to until Henrietta told her to find answers at Villa Prep. Things just keep spiraling out of control. I don't know what the right thing to do is. And trying to cover up her murdering Jerome ..."

"First of all, how do you know he was murdered, and secondly, who murdered Jerome Bonovich?"

Toby and I both turned to see Dad standing behind us with his arms crossed over his chest.

Shit.

CHAPTER TWENTY-SEVEN

Toby

Dad allowed us to shower and get changed before meeting him in the living room to tell him everything we knew. He took our phones so we couldn't text anyone and dared us to try to sneak out of the house. He wasn't above tasing his own sons.

I was the last to get a shower, so I was the last to make it to the living room where he waited with Rush. I tried to think of a way out of this, but there wasn't one. He heard what was said, and there was no going back now.

As soon as I took a seat next to my brother, Dad stood. "Now, tell me everything, and if you hold something back and I find out about it, I promise to make you wish you had just told me."

"Jorja killed Jerome Bonovich," Rush said quietly.

I glared at him. He didn't have to break that easily. I mean, I knew we'd have to just come clean at some point, but damn.

Dad closed his eyes and sighed heavily. "And?" he asked, pinching the bridge of his nose.

"We helped her get rid of the body," Rush said quickly. When I glared at him again, he threw his hands up. "What? Might as well get it over with. Rip it off like a Band-Aid."

Dad looked at me. "Toby, is this true?"

"What if I said it wasn't, and I must've punched Rush too hard and he wasn't thinking straight?"

Dad crossed his arms. "I'd appreciate the truth."

I nodded. "Yes, sir. It's the truth."

"Do you both realize how bad this is?" He started yelling and cursing so loudly, his words became unintelligible.

I stared at the floor as he continued to yell. There was no point in interrupting him or trying to make this better. It'd never be better. It was extremely screwed up and always would be.

"So, what do we do? Do we turn ourselves in?" Rush asked.

I looked up from the floor, waiting for the answer.

"I don't know, but I have to make a decision fast. If it comes out that Jorja murdered him, she will immediately be taken into custody. If I can get her to say she acted alone—"

"No," I stated firmly. "She won't go down alone."

"I agree," Rush added.

Dad groaned as he sat in the recliner. "I have never, in seventeen years of working as a police officer, covered up a crime. I vowed I wouldn't." He closed his eyes, took a deep breath, let it out, and looked at us. "Dammit."

Rush and I both remained silent while Dad battled with his thoughts.

"How did she kill him?" he asked.

I guess Rush was tired of answering questions because he looked at me to answer.

"Poisoned his drink," I answered.

"And how exactly were you two involved?"

I felt Rush's eyes on me. I rubbed the tension in my forehead and sighed heavily. "We helped her get rid of the body."

"Where?" he asked through clenched teeth.

I looked at my hands. "Somewhere in the river." I shrugged. "I don't have the exact directions. We just dropped it in and left."

Multiple curse words left his mouth. Rush and I watched as he paced the living room floor. I felt bad that I was putting Dad through this, but I didn't regret helping Jorja, no matter what amount of trouble I was in.

"What's going to happen to us?" Rush asked quietly. Even though we had both taken showers and cleaned up, our faces still looked like we had been hit by a truck. I liked to think he looked worse than me, though.

Dad stopped pacing and stood in front of us. "Nothing. I would have never thought my boys would be tied up in some mess like this, but here we are. I'll die protecting this secret, but you better not tell a soul. I will speak to Jorja myself about the importance of this remaining a secret. I will find a way to get the search back going again, maybe say it's from an anonymous person giving possible details. I'll figure it out. Either way people need to know he's dead."

"But it might not be him," Rush added, causing Dad's eyes to widen.

"What do you mean?" he asked.

Rush looked at me before continuing. "I mean, it's possible that Jerome has a twin and he could've been there that night. Jorja swears she saw him or someone who looked like him the night she was shot."

I gave Rush a warning look, hoping he'd stop talking. I didn't know how much Jorja wanted out in the open, and Dad had already found out enough.

Rush didn't pay any attention to me and focused on Dad.

He slowly sat in the recliner. "This just keeps getting better and better."

"Jorja doesn't know this for sure, though. It could honestly be delusion from the shock of being shot," I added.

Dad leaned back into the chair and closed his eyes. "Right now," he said, opening his eyes, "I just want you two to just keep going on as you normally would. We can't act like anything is different or it will raise suspicion. When I figure out how to handle this, I will keep you two informed."

Rush and I both nodded.

"Go get some sleep," he said to the both of us.

After telling Dad goodnight, we both headed to our rooms without a word to one another.

CHAPTER TWENTY-EIGHT

Jorja

I was notified by Henrietta that a new driver was hired to escort me to and from Villa Prep and he would be waiting on me this morning. When I walked outside, I almost cried. I was so happy to see Mr. Bill, the gatekeeper of Grove Hills, standing next to the limo.

"Miss Bonovich," he said, tipping his hat.

I ran to him and hugged him. "How did you get this job?" I asked as I pulled away.

He chuckled and opened the back door for me. "Your grandmother and I are old friends. She can be very convincing, but it didn't take much when she told me who I'd be driving."

"Are you not working for the Grove Hills gated community anymore?"

"I'll still be working night shifts there." He motioned for me to get into the car.

I put my backpack in first and then slid into the seat. I watched as he closed the door and got into the driver's seat. The window that separated the back to the front was open, and I moved up so I could rest my arms on the ledge where the window came through and smiled at him in the rearview mirror.

"What'd you mean by my grandmother and you are old friends?"

He started driving and smiled. "We went to Villa Prep together. I know your grandparents very well. Never liked your grandfather, though."

I felt like there was a big story there and decided to test my luck at finding it out. "Why?"

He laughed. "That's a long story."

"I had no idea you knew my family like this, or went to Villa Prep. No offense, but usually the big names go to Villa Prep and don't end up working as gatekeepers."

He laughed some more with a slight nod of his head. "This is true. I had aspirations to be a commercial pilot, actually went into the Air Force and was going to pursue my dream job after my service, but I was contacted by your grandmother to come work for the gated community."

"You work for my family?"

"Yes and no."

My brow furrowed. "What do you mean?"

"I took the job as a favor for your family."

"But why? What is the favor?"

His smile faded as he watched the road ahead of him. "Keeping their secrets."

"And it sounds like you owed my grandmother a favor."

His smile returned. "At one point in my life, I was in love with your grandmother until she left me for your grandfather. He was bad news, still is."

"But you told me you were happily married."

"And I was, and I miss my late wife every single day. You always love your first love, though."

My mind was immediately filled with thoughts of Toby. Not Rush. I ignored that realization before going back to the conversation with Mr. Bill. "Did she choose my grandfather over you?"

"Something like that."

"Why are you telling me all of this?" I asked, genuinely confused but grateful.

"Because I'm on your side, too, Jorja. We're going to bring down the Bonovich family."

Chills crept all over my skin. "You know?"

"I know everything."

Tears filled my eyes. "And you want to help me?"

"It's been the plan all along."

"All along?" I asked.

"Since the moment we found out you weren't Jerome's baby."

"We?"

He looked at me through the rearview mirror. "Your grandmother and me. Your mother came to her when she first found out she was pregnant with you."

"Our conversation isn't being recorded here, is it?"

He shook his head as he watched the road. "No. The car is tapped, but I can turn it on and off. Your grandfather doesn't know that, though."

It was then that I noticed his Southern drawl wasn't there anymore. "Didn't you have a Southern accent?"

"All an act."

I wasn't alone in wanting to bring the family down. Henrietta, Mr. Bill, Olivia, Peter, Mr. Ellison, Toby, Rush, my friends ... They all wanted to see the Bonovich name burn. The next question was risking so much because what if Mr. Bill was lying? What if he was really on Jacob's side? In my gut, I knew he was telling me the truth, but there was always that chance he wasn't.

Going into the school felt as if I were standing at the edge of a cliff and someone came behind me and pushed. I didn't hear the dean of students the first time he addressed me, so, with a bit of frustration, he cleared his throat and repeated himself.

"Miss Bonovich, I am Dean Herst, head of Villa Preparatory. We welcome you to the most prestigious education establishment in Colorado." It was obvious he had practiced that line.

I shook his hand. "It's nice to meet you. It's an honor to be here." I looked around at the entrance of the huge historical building. "This place is beautiful." The pitched ceilings plated in gold, the mahogany paneled walls shined to perfection, and marble floors were honestly breathtaking. It reminded me of the historic charm of our home in Grove Hills.

"Your family are great financial contributors to this institution. I was actually shocked you haven't started here sooner like your brother and sister did."

"I'm the odd duck, I guess." I smiled sheepishly and looked at a group of girls passing me as they whispered amongst one another. I instantly missed my friends.

"I'm very sorry about the recent loss of your brother and your missing father. We have an excellent school counselor that is available at any time to you." He motioned for me to follow him.

He spoke about the history of the school as I followed him up a flight of stairs. At some point, he had handed me my schedule, but I was too busy to realize it as I took in everything. I already felt out of place. I didn't belong here. I was only being treated with respect because of a last name that wasn't actually mine.

But, according to my grandmother, there were answers there, and I was going to find them.

I'd play the game.

I'd get the answers.

Whatever there was there for me to find had to be good if Henrietta risked everything to tell me she was on my side.

CHAPTER TWENTY-NINE

Rush

"Are you okay?" Tommy asked me as we sat down for lunch.

I pushed my food away. "I've been better. Why?" My entire body was sore from the fight with Toby, and my mind raced with thoughts about the conversation Toby and I had with Dad.

"Okay," Beck said, placing his plate down beside me and taking a seat, "tell me what the hell happened to you and Toby. Did you have a wreck?"

Only Tommy knew what happened, but I knew I'd have to tell everyone at some point.

"Me and my brother had a fight," I admitted and then had everyone's attention.

"Over what?" Wren asked.

"Idiot. Jorja, of course. It was bound to happen," Jena said, rolling her eyes. She was mad Toby didn't want anything to do with her.

Becca looked at her phone. "Jorja told me about it." She looked at me again. "How are we supposed to help Jorja if you two are fighting over her?"

I shrugged. "We're not fighting over her anymore."

"What does that mean?" Tommy asked.

I looked at him. "It means exactly what I said. If her and Toby choose to be together, then that's what she chooses. If she chooses me, then she does. Right now, helping her is what's important, not putting her in the middle of a fight between my brother and me."

"Now that she's going to that private school, we're going to have to get more strategic about how we see her," Becca said.

I looked at her. "We can go to her grandparents'. She knows places we can talk safely."

I looked at my phone when it dinged.

Peter: I know I'm the last person you want to talk to, but we need to talk. Can you meet after school?

I hadn't heard from Peter since breaking his nose when he did all of those things to Jorja after I told him to stop. Toby mentioned he and Jorja's sister were working together to help Jorja, so I did want to see what he had to say.

Me: Where do you want to meet?
Peter: My house at 4:00.
Me: I'll be there.

I looked at Tommy. "That was Peter. He wants to talk."

"Want me to go with you?"

I nodded.

We all spent the rest of lunch eating in silence. Without Jorja, things felt off. I wondered how things might be different had I never connected with Peter and the plan to bring Jorja's family down never happened. Jorja could've lived peacefully in the lies. Brian would still be alive. She could've gone on believing Jerome was her father. If it weren't for me wanting to avenge my mother's death, none of this would've happened.

Tommy and I pulled into Peter's driveway and parked. I couldn't help but look at Jorja's house that sat on the highest hill, overlooking the rest of the subdivision. Tommy nudged me to get my attention and motioned toward Peter's house. I saw him coming out of the front door. I put my hands into my pockets and leaned against Tommy's car.

"I didn't know you were bringing anyone," Peter said, eyeing Tommy.

"I don't think you're in a place where you get to worry about that," Tommy snapped back.

"I deserved that," Peter said, looking down at his shoes. He looked at me. "Let's go inside. We don't need to talk out here."

Tommy and I followed him inside. His mom, Mrs. Judy, greeted us with a warm smile as she cut up carrots at the large island in the middle of the kitchen.

"Rush, it's been a while since I've seen you. How are you?"

We stopped walking, and I went and gave her a hug. "Good. You're looking as beautiful as ever."

She laughed. "I already told you, I'm too old for you," she teased.

"Mr. Ellison knows you're really married to me. It's okay to tell the truth now," I teased back. This family was such a good family. They always made me feel welcome, and I'd be lying if I said I didn't miss them.

She laughed some more. "Are you boys staying for dinner?" She looked at Tommy. "And you are?"

He held his hand out. "Tommy McCarthey."

Mrs. Judy wiped her hands on a towel and shook his hand. "Doesn't your dad own Grove Hills Bank?"

Tommy nodded. "Yes, ma'am."

Her smile widened. "I know your family, then. Good people."

Tommy's nose crinkled as he looked at her after that statement. He wasn't a fan of his family at all. Judy went back to cutting carrots.

"We didn't plan on staying long," I said, bringing the conversation back to the dinner offer.

"Well, if you boys change your mind, there's plenty."

"Thank you," I said, before we followed Peter to his room.

Once we were inside the room, Peter shut the door. "I've been working with Jorja's sister to find out enough to present a case to a private detective that has been following the Bonoviches criminal activity for a few years now. My dad is working with a lawyer and has already spoke with the judge about all of this. Once we have proof of things, we can move forward with filing everything and getting Jorja out of there and here with us, if she wants to be here."

My eyes narrowed. "Have you asked Jorja about any of this?"

He shook his head. "No. I figured she wouldn't want to talk to me, but I know you're close to her, and I figured she would listen to you and you could arrange for us to meet and discuss all of this."

"She also listens to her sister. Why not send Olivia to talk to her?"

"Because Olivia has to stay hidden. This is the best way."

Tommy remained quiet.

"I hope you all know who you're messing with. This family is lethal. They kill with zero remorse to protect their agendas," I said gravely.

Peter nodded. "I know. It's why they killed your mom."

"They killed my mom because she owed a debt she couldn't repay."

Peter's eyes saddened. "No, Rush. They killed your mom because she was going to the authorities because they were forcing her to sell, and she didn't want to. She wanted to quit using drugs. She wanted to be healthy and sober for you and Toby. They kept her addicted, they manipulated her like a puppet because she had major connections to big time buyers."

Tears burned my eyes. "What? How do you know this?"

"Olivia has been spying for a long time, waiting for a weak spot in their schemes to finally bring them down. Your mother's death, Jerome missing, all of it has created the perfect time to take them down. She reached out to me because she knew my family cares for Jorja, and we want nothing more than that family to pay for what they've done. She has proof, records, and recordings of Jerome having conversations with your mother."

I wanted to ask if she ever mentioned Jerome being a twin, but my emotions were spiraling, and it was hard to form words. I hoped we killed the right man because the satisfaction of seeing the body slip deep into the depths of the river felt even better now. And if he wasn't dead and Jorja killed the wrong man, I'd find Jerome myself.

I fought back the sobs threatening to escape, and my words came out thick. "I'll talk to Jorja."

"Let me know when she can meet with me. We have a lot to talk about."

Tommy looked at Peter. "You better be serious about all of this. You're lucky Rush only broke your nose for what you did to Jorja."

Peter laughed. "Trust me, I'm not proud of what I did, but to be honest, I really thought I was doing the right thing. I never meant to hurt Jorja, but when I found out what the family did and how they kept her away from us ... I just had enough. When I finally get to talk to her, I promise I will apologize. I'll make it right."

My head was all over the place, and I needed to leave before I broke down. "I'll text you when I talk to her."

After we left, Tommy drove me to my truck I had left parked at the school. I didn't talk the entire car ride, and Tommy respected that by not saying anything. Mom was forced to abide by their rules. My imagination ran wild with all of the possible things that could've meant. She wanted to be clean. She didn't want to do drugs, but they forced them on her. They let her life spiral so out of control, and it ultimately led her to being murdered, leaving her kids behind. I wondered what Toby would do with this information. He always thought Mom freely made the choice to be a shitty parent and drug addict. Maybe he could forgive her now.

CHAPTER THIRTY

Toby

I FaceTimed Jorja, hoping she'd answer. I just needed to see her and see for myself she survived her first day at the new school. When she answered, her smile lit my soul on fire.

"Hey," she said softly. She was lying in her bed, and it looked like she was still in her uniform from school. The navy blazer made her eyes a deeper shade of blue.

"How was Villa?"

She scrunched her nose, making a disgusted face.

I laughed. "That bad, huh?"

"It was mostly figuring out where I was supposed to go all day. The dean of students made me meet with the counselor, too. I didn't eat lunch in the cafeteria today, I ate in the library while they assigned me all of my books. There are *so* many books."

"And the other students were nice?"

She shrugged. "I was so busy just trying to navigate the huge building and get information from the teachers that I didn't pay attention to anyone else. I missed all of you, though. That was torture."

"The entire school is talking about you not being there. It's like the universe's balance is off."

She laughed. "I'm sure a majority are celebrating in my wake."

"No one was celebrating."

She didn't say anything for a moment and just stared at me. "Is Rush mad at me?"

"Why would Rush be mad at you?"

She chewed on her lip. "I told him I have feelings for you. And him. He asked me, and I couldn't lie, Toby. I haven't heard from him at all today."

"I think you should talk to Rush about Rush. Not me."

She sighed sadly. "Sorry. You're right."

"I know all of this is confusing for you."

"It is, but it's not fair for you or him. I wish I wasn't putting either of you through this, but I also can't lie or deny how I feel. Everything is so messed up. I don't want to hurt anyone."

I watched as a tear slipped down her cheek and wished I was there to wipe it away. I hated that I allowed myself to fall for a girl who fell for two people in the midst of her own hell. She was right, it wasn't fair, but I willingly made the choice to pursue things with her. I wished I could selfishly convince her to choose me and allow me to be the one she ran to when everything became too much.

"If I could make decisions for you to help, I would."

She laughed and wiped her eyes. "So you'd choose you for me."

"No," I said seriously. "So I could choose what makes you happy."

"I wish I could just run away, but the truth is, even if I did, this life would always haunt me."

I needed to tell her that my dad knew about her killing Jerome and Rush and me helping, but tonight wasn't a good night. It'd have to wait for now.

"Unfortunately, running away from our problems never works."

She brushed some hair out of her face and met my eyes. "Can I ask you a serious question?"

I nodded.

"Do you honestly see a future with me, if you and I were to work out? Because I'm struggling to see what anyone could see in me but trouble. How does anyone who knows anything about me and what I've been through see anything other than this broken girl who is the product of scandal?" She spoke low, I'm sure to conceal her voice from any possibly listening ears.

Just as I was about to answer, there was a knock on my bedroom door.

"Toby, it's Rush. I need to talk to you now." The urgency in his voice caused me to get up and open the door for him. I looked at Jorja on the phone. "I'll call you back. Sorry." I hung up after she told me bye and stepped back to let Rush into the room.

"Mom wanted to quit! She tried, but they wouldn't let her!" He spoke so quickly it was almost hard to understand what he was saying.

"Slow down. What are you talking about?"

Tears streamed down his cheeks. "We were wrong about Mom. Those monsters kept her addicted and forced her to sell their drugs. She wanted out but her life was on the line. She was going to tell everything, but they found out and killed her!"

"How'd you find all of this out?"

He wiped his eyes on the back of his hand. "Peter. He and Olivia found all of this out. They are working on gathering enough proof to turn it in."

Mom was scared, but that didn't change the fact that she got involved with the Bonoviches in the first place. At one point she initially started doing drugs. She made that choice, and it spiraled into more than she bargained for. It was still her fault, and my mind wouldn't change.

"Rush, she still got herself into that mess. This changes nothing for me."

"Because you're selfish!" he shouted.

"Call me what you want, but I did not have the same relationship with her like you did. She chose you because of a stupid birthmark that matched hers. I have always been second best to her. Dad hated the arrangement but wanted to keep the divorce as peaceful as possible."

"She loved you, Toby."

I shook my head. "Not enough. Anyone can love someone, but actions will always speak louder. I don't doubt she loved me, but she didn't love me or you more than the drugs. She wanted out, which is good, but if she had never gotten involved there would have been no need for all she went through and she wouldn't be rotting in the damn ground."

Rush's tears calmed and so did his breathing. "I hate that you're right." He sat down on my bed.

"I wish that I wasn't." I leaned against the wall.

"We are way over our heads with all of this."

I nodded. "And we still need to tell Jorja Dad knows."

"Yeah ... I need to text her and ask her about her day."

I wanted to comment that I already talked to her but didn't.

CHAPTER THIRTY-ONE

Jorja

The whispers and stares were worse at Villa Prep today. Or maybe I was just paying more attention than I did yesterday. I had just made it past a group of girls staring and quietly saying my name when I ran into a really tall guy that felt like a brick wall.

"I'm so sorry!" I said quickly.

His preppy persona made me regret ever being the way I was at Grove. Everything about him screamed self-absorbed. His laugh was surprisingly pleasant, though.

"You're actually exactly who I was looking for. It appears that the universe has delivered you to me herself."

The difference in height made it an easy shot if I wanted to kick him in the balls. "I'm not being delivered to anyone." I went to walk past him, but he moved swiftly to block me.

"I'm Bentley Herrington."

"And I didn't ask." I went to walk past him again, but he was quick to block me once more. I sighed heavily.

He laughed. "You're eating lunch with us today."

"I'm not one to be told what to do."

"Okay, will you *please* eat lunch with us today?"

"No," I snapped. "And I need to get to class before I'm late."

"Just tell them you were with me. They won't argue."

My stomach churned at his arrogance. "Move, Bentley."

"Can't wait to see you at lunch," he said as he moved to the side, laughing. "By the way," he said, causing me to stop walking, "your grandmother told me to protect you here at Villa, and I'll do just that even if you don't want me to."

"How do you know my grandmother?"

"We'll talk later. Don't want you to be late for class." He winked before walking off.

Extremely irritated, I had forgotten where I was supposed to go. I pulled out my schedule and headed toward history class.

Skipping lunch and hiding in the library sounded like a way better idea than going to find Bentley, but if my grandmother truly asked him to look out for me here, I needed to know why. I was told I'd find answers here and maybe Bentley Herrington had them.

I looked around the cafeteria that looked more like a fancy dining hall. Food was being brought out by waitresses and drinks being poured by waiters. The tables were decorated with large floral arrangements and the lights were low, creating a calming ambience. I couldn't deny the food smelled and looked amazing even if I hated everything about this and missed the chaos of Grove High.

As I looked around, not finding Bentley anywhere, I felt a hand on my shoulder. I looked up to see him. "Don't touch me," I warned.

He smiled, not at all fazed by my demand. "We sit over there," he said, removing his hand and pointing toward a circular table toward the exit.

I followed him to the table where two girls and two other guys sat. The girls stared at me like I was a threat, and the guys looked at me like I was a puzzle to be put back together. Bentley reached for my bag. Confused, I just held it tighter.

"I was just going to take it and set it down for you." He chuckled. "This is Jorja Bonovich. I expect nothing short of a warm welcome for our new friend."

"We're not friends," I snapped.

He started introducing me to everyone rather than commenting on my remark. "This is Angela Thompson," he said, pointing to the girl with jet black hair cut into a perfect bob. She waved with a little smile. He then pointed to the girl next to her with long red hair and a face covered in freckles. "This is Temper Block," he said, laughing as she rolled her eyes.

"It's not really Temper, that's my nickname. They like to tease me about my hair and say I have a red-headed temper. My name is Kelcey." Her greens eyes narrowed at Bentley. "Shall we introduce Bentley? The biggest dick in the entire school?" The girls burst into laughter.

Bentley's shoulders shook with laughter. "Anyway," he said, turning his attention to the other two guys. He pointed at the short chubby one with blonde curls. "That's Bradley Nelson," and as he continued, he pointed at the last guy whose eyes were basically hidden under his shaggy sandy-blonde hair, "and that's Chris Roberson."

Bradley and Chris acknowledged their introductions with a slight nod of their heads.

Bentley pulled out a chair and motioned for me to sit. After I sat down, he took the seat next to me. I had never felt so out of place in my life. I pulled out my phone to text the group chat with all of my friends.

Me: I miss you guys.

Messages from everyone came flooding in saying how much they missed me too. I put the phone in my backpack before putting the bag on the floor beside my chair.

"It's an honor to have a Bonovich in our presence," Bentley said as food was placed in front of us.

I wanted to take my plate and go hide.

Angela took a bite of her food and looked at me. After taking a drink of her water, she spoke. "Why are you going here now?"

Kelcey groaned. "Why are you asking her something the entire school already knows? Her father is missing, she was shot and almost killed; it makes sense her grandparents enrolled her here where she is a lot safer than with the commons."

The commons? That comment made my blood boil. "None of you here are better than anyone because you attend this snobby school."

Kelcey scoffed at my comment. "We are better. We are far superior, and if you don't see that, then you're just in denial."

"It's facts, sweetheart," Chris stated calmly. "If we weren't, we wouldn't be able to afford to attend Villa. The sooner you accept that reality, the better."

"You're all sick," I said as I stood. I grabbed my things, left the dining hall, and headed to the library. I knew I needed to figure out Bentley, but I wouldn't do it at the expense of my morals or sanity.

I had just made it to the library when I noticed Bentley had followed me the entire way.

"What?" I snapped as I turned to face him.

He held two plates of food in his hands. "I'm sorry about what happened. I know that comment Kelcey made upset you because she was talking about your friends."

I tried to ignore him and sat at a small table near the large windows. He sat across from me and slid the plate in my direction. I looked at the food and then at him.

"How do you know my grandmother?"

"My parents are very close with your family. I've been at a lot of the parties your parents have hosted, but you usually were with your friends or hiding somewhere."

"My grandmother never said anything about you, so why would she ask you to protect me here?"

He moved the food around on his plate as he thought. After taking a bite and swallowing, he looked at me again. "Because people here don't accept new students very well. She wanted me to be sure you got in with us so no one would mess with you. And we all have something in common."

"Who is all?"

"Temper, Angela, Chris, Bradley, and me."

I narrowed my eyes at him. "What could we possibly have in common?"

"We're all taking a part in the family business when we graduate."

That comment made it obvious he didn't know everything, and it had to stay that way. My grandmother had to have wanted me to make a connection with him because being around him would help me get the answers I needed. He was an important part of the game I was playing. The whole group was.

"We're all going into the same thing, so we'd have to be friends at some point."

I raised a brow. "The same thing?"

He laughed. "Don't play like you don't know. I wouldn't talk about something like this with someone who wasn't involved. We're future business partners, Jorja. We protect each other." He pointed to my food. "You should eat."

I watched as he started eating and felt sorry for him. I felt sorry for all five of them. But I wasn't sorry that I'd use them to get the answers I needed. Feeling sorry and being sorry were two totally different things.

CHAPTER THIRTY-TWO

Rush

I was pulling a Toby and came to Jorja's grandparents' without telling him. I didn't tell anyone, actually—not even Jorja. I came here straight after school and waited at the gate for her to pull in. When I saw the limo in my rearview mirror, I got out of the truck and smiled as the limo got closer. It came to a slow stop, and she got out of the car.

"Rush!" she squealed and ran over to me. She hugged me. "What are you doing here?"

"I wanted to come see you. Look at your cute little uniform," I said, taking her hand and spinning her in a slow circle.

She laughed. "It's nothing special."

"Can I steal you for a bit?"

She looked over her shoulder at the driver of the limo before looking back at me. "I can't leave."

"What if no one finds out?"

She chewed on her bottom lip as she thought. "Let me ask Mr. Bill."

"Mr. Bill? The gatekeeper at Grove Hills?"

She grinned. "Yup! Be right back."

I watched as she went to the driver's side, and he rolled down the window. She talked to him and waited while he made a phone call. When he pulled the phone away from his ear he nodded, and she came back over.

"Let's go, but I have to be back no later than eight."

We got into my truck, and I started driving back down the long drive. "How did you get permission?"

"Mr. Bill and Grandmother are close friends."

"Okay, wait, so you're calling her Grandmother again and not just Henrietta?"

I shrugged. "I don't really know. I've called her Grandmother for so long, and maybe she deserves the title after all."

"Now that she says she's on your side?"

She nodded and looked out the window. "Where are we going?"

"Want to go to the lake?"

Her smile widened. "So much."

"Your boulder has missed you."

She laughed as she looked at me. "I've missed *you*, Rush."

I believed her, but I also couldn't get past her admitting to me she had feelings for my brother, too. I respected her for her honesty, but it still hurt. I wouldn't let it ruin my mood, though. I finally got to spend time with her, and I wouldn't mess it up.

"I missed you, too."

When I pulled into our spot at the lake, I stopped her before she got out of the truck. "I need to tell you something."

Her smile faded. "You look upset."

"Well, I'm nervous to tell you."

"What is it?" She folded her hands on her lap.

"My dad knows you killed Jerome and Toby and me helped get rid of the body."

Her eyes widened. "Oh, no."

I nodded. "Yeah ... he's pissed we didn't tell him sooner, but he's going to cover for us. He did say he wants to talk to you, though."

"What do you mean cover for us? Does someone suspect us?"

I shook my head. "No. Just if they do."

She looked at her hands. "Your dad probably hates me."

"He doesn't hate you."

She looked at me again. "Who told him?" She looked angry now.

"Well ... technically, I did, but he overheard Toby and me talking."

Her eyes went to my bruised eye before saying anything. "And what happens if he can't keep it a secret?"

"He will," I said with certainty. "Jorja, you can trust him." I needed to tell her Peter wanted to talk to her, too, but I didn't know how after hitting her with the news about Dad knowing.

She got out of the truck without saying anything and went to sit on the huge boulder she'd claimed as hers. I killed the engine and got out of the truck. She stared off into the distance, lost in thought. I didn't know if I should go sit with her or not. If she wanted me to, she would've mentioned it, so I went and stood near the spot where we have bonfires. Maybe I should've waited to break the news to her or let Toby do it. I finally got the chance to be alone with her, and now I felt further away from her than I had before.

The distance was killing me, so I went over to her and stood in front of her. She looked at me, but her eyes remained cold.

"What are you thinking?" I asked, bracing myself for her to yell at me. I should've never told Dad. Toby and I could've come up with a lie. We could have covered it up, and we didn't. No, *I* didn't. Toby wasn't speaking. I spoke up first. She needed to know that, but I selfishly didn't tell her.

"About turning myself in." She laughed forcefully, like a joke had been told and it wasn't funny at all. "Everyone's trying to protect me. From what? From who? Is Jerome a twin or not? Did I even kill the right man? Who all is lying to me or telling me the truth. I'm exhausted. I'm sick and tired of living this hell every single day. I miss my brother. I need to talk to him so bad, but he's dead! He's dead because—"

"Of me!" I shouted. "He's dead because of me and Peter devising this whole plan to bring your family down. If we wouldn't have done that, Peter wouldn't have kept on, and you could have lived peacefully in your lies and secrets, and everything would be normal!"

"Until someone else outed it all. Olivia has been working on it. She told Toby to tell me to stop and let her handle it. No matter what, this is my life, Rush. This is who I am, and no matter how long I live, I will never escape it. There is no future for me. I might as well be behind bars. I'm safer there, and everyone will be safer without me around."

I shook my head adamantly. "No. That doesn't fix anything. My mother was going to out your family. Did you know that?"

"How do you know that?"

"I talked to Peter. He wants to talk to you," I said, deciding to drop that bomb since we were already discussing everything. "He asked me to tell you that and figure out if you would or not. His dad, your real father, wants to save you from all of this. He's fighting for you. Turning yourself in won't help anything. I promised you I wouldn't go to the police about seeing Jerome kill my mother, now you promise me you won't turn yourself in."

Tears filled her eyes as she looked past me and stared into the distance. She cursed quietly and looked at me again. "Fine. I won't." She wiped her cheeks on the sleeve of her blazer. "When can I talk to Peter?"

"When do you want to?"

"What time is it?"

I looked at my phone. "Almost five."

"Think he can talk now?"

"Are you sure you want to? I mean, it can wait if you need time."

She hopped off the boulder and started walking to my truck. "I'm fine. Let's go."

I caught up with her and pulled up Peter's contact in my phone. "Let me call him and make sure he's—"

"Tell him he doesn't have a choice. I'm going now. I don't know the next time I'll be able to sneak away." She kept walking until she made it to my truck and got in.

I called Peter as I got in on the driver's side.

"Hey," I said as soon as he answered. "I have Jorja with me, and she is adamant that we come now."

"Now?"

"Yeah, now." I looked over at Jorja as she stared out the window.

"My parents are here. Does she want me to meet you both somewhere?"

"Peter asked if you want to go there or he could meet us somewhere," I asked her. "His parents are home."

She looked at me with an expression that was hard to read. "There is fine."

"We're coming there."

"I'll let my parents know." He hung up, and I set my phone on the dash.

"Are you sure this is a good idea to go right now? Just a second ago—"

"What is considered a good idea anymore, Rush?" she asked, cutting me off. "If I wait to talk to him, it's not a good idea. If I talk to him now, it's not a good idea. So, I'm going now."

She had a point, but I still worried her emotions would spiral out of control. "Okay. We're going." I put the truck in reverse, backed out of the spot I was parked in, then headed toward town.

CHAPTER THIRTY-THREE

Toby

I needed to tell Jorja something, but I didn't know how. I had been keeping a secret from everyone, even Rush. I pushed it so far into the inner compartments of my memory that I wouldn't think about it at all. The last time I thought about this was the night in the garden with everyone and swore I wouldn't think about it again, but, today, it was all I could think about.

I failed.

I tried to kill him, and it didn't work, but I knew I hit him.

When he killed our mother, the pain he caused my brother, I wanted him dead.

I should've looked the night we sent his body to the depths of the water. If I had known it'd be suspected Jermone had a twin, I would've confirmed there was a bullet wound on the right side of his chest.

My door burst open, and Dad came rushing in. "Have you heard from Jorja?"

"No? Why?"

"I got a call that her house is on fire in Grove Hills."

"What!" I sat up and stood from the bed, quickly putting on my shoes.

"You can ride with me. I called your brother, but he didn't answer."

I followed him out of the house and listened as he talked on the radio. I could hear the dispatcher sending out the cops and fire department. I tried calling Jorja several times, but she never answered.

Panic set in.

She was with her grandparents. She wouldn't have been there. She wasn't allowed to be there.

I called again. Still no answer.

I decided to try Rush next, and he answered on the third ring.

"Please tell me you're with Jorja," I said quickly.

"I'm with her. We just pulled up at Peter's so they could talk and next thing we know there's smoke and flames. Jorja tried to go, but we have her here with us. Mr. Ellison is trying to talk some sense into her. She's worried her mom is in there."

"We're not far. I'll have Dad drop me off at Peter's." I hung up the phone. "Drop me off at Peter's. Jorja and Rush are there."

His eyebrows shot up. "She's at her real dad's?"

"Apparently. But she's safe. I'll ask questions later."

When we pulled into the gated community, Dad rolled down his window, showed his badge to the gatekeeper, and we were let in. He quickly dropped me off at Peter's, and as he drove off, I went to the door.

Before I could knock, Rush opened the door. "I was watching for you."

"Where is she?"

"Follow me," he opened the door all the way to let me in, and I followed him into the living room where they had Jorja sitting on the couch, guarding her just in case she tried to make a run for it.

As soon as her eyes found me, she started crying. "Toby, tell them to let me go! My mom could be in there! She isn't answering her phone and—" I cut her off by sitting by her and hugging her, rubbing her back gently.

"You can't go in there. You have to let the professionals handle this now," I spoke softly against her ear as I continued to hold her close. Her entire body trembled, so I held her tighter until I felt the trembling stop. I moved back and took her hand in mine. She leaned against me, burying her face against my chest.

I looked up to see everyone in the room watching us. Rush's jaw tensed, and he looked away. Mr. Ellison's phone rang, and he stepped out of the room to answer it. She held so tightly to my hand it started tingling, but I'd allow her to cut off the blood supply if it soothed her worries at all.

"I'm going to protect you forever," I whispered against her ear. "Even if you don't want me to."

I was unapologetically in love with this girl. To hell with my sanity. I'd bury the logical part of my brain for her every single time. Rush could glare at me, yell at me, hit me, I didn't care. Even if she never said she was mine, she'd always be just that in my head. Delusion, if that's what it was, was my new euphoria.

Her eyes met mine, begging me, and I was listening. "I need to be there."

Fuck it.

I stood and held her hand as she rose to her feet. "I'm taking her to get some air."

"Toby—" Rush's words faltered as we made our way outside despite everyone's warnings against it.

Once outside, we picked up our pace, jogging up the hill to the house. Firefighters worked tirelessly to extinguish the flames but failed. It was too late. The house was gone. Once the focal point of Grove Hills was now a pile of ash. Jorja grabbed my arm, digging her nails into it as tears streamed down her cheeks.

She gasped when she saw her mom clutching to a metal box and being put into my dad's cop car. Before shutting the door, Dad took the box from her though she screamed for him to give it back. Her bellowing was muffled once the door was closed. Dad looked at Jorja and me, shook his head sadly, and got into his car.

Jorja turned to me, and even though she was clearly shaken by seeing her home destroyed and her mother being taken away, her words didn't shock me. "I need to get that box."

CHAPTER THIRTY-FOUR

Jorja

I sat in the waiting area at the police station with Toby on my right and Rush on my left. All of my friends sat scattered around the waiting room. The walls felt like they were closing in on me, and my breaths felt forced and narrow. My mother was being accused of arson. Something she said led them to believe she did it, but according to Officer True, she denied she ever said that and they misheard her.

Why was I even there?

I didn't understand my feelings when it came to my mother at all. I loved her, but I hated her. I trusted her, yet I didn't trust her at all. The oxymoron of our relationship confused the hell out of me.

Did she do it?

Probably.

Why?

Many reasons.

Was she hiding something?

She hid everything.

If she did it, who was she trying to save? Who was she protecting? Or maybe she had too much wine mixed with pills and she went into a manic state where she wanted it all gone. Maybe she didn't start it at all.

But ... what was in the box she clutched to her chest? Watching her scream as Officer True pried it from her hands made me want nothing more than to get my hands on it. It was property of the Grove Hills Police Department now. Toby agreed to help me get it, but Rush told me to leave it alone.

I looked up when Becca came over to me. "Jorja, can I get you something to drink? Or eat?"

I shook my head.

We all turned when Officer True came through the door.

"Can I talk to her?" I asked for the millionth time. I'd been asking that same question since we gotten there an hour ago.

"Yes, you can now." I stood and followed him through the door and down the long hallway.

We went into the door at the very end of the hall on the right. It was exactly like the movies. A cold, dimly lit room with a metal table and two chairs in the middle. My mother sat at the far side, and her eyes were locked on mine.

Officer True pulled the chair across from her and motioned for me to sit. I sat down and watched as he went to stand near the door. They had my mother handcuffed to the table like she was some monster ready to attack. What had she done?

"Mom, what's going on?" My voice sounded weak, and I hated myself for it.

Her pupils were heavily dilated, indicating she was definitely on something. "It's all happening now."

"What's happening?"

"Everything," she whispered.

"What do you mean everything?"

She laughed maniacally. "Don't you see, Jorja? This is all happening because of you."

My chest tightened, and my heart started to beat faster. "I don't understand. What is because of me?"

"You were a mistake! Your birth rattled the bones of the entire thing. You've screwed it all up! You shouldn't exist! If it weren't for you, Jerome would still be here. Olivia would still be here! Your brother would still be here!" she screamed and banged her fist on the table, the chains rattling from the force.

My whole body began to tremble. I felt my bottom lip quiver, tears daring to fall, but I willed them back. Officer True came over, urging me to get up as my mother continued to scream. I stood, my legs shaking making it hard to take a step forward. Officer True placed his hand on my back, steadying me as he hurried me out of the room. He shut the door, locked it, and as I began to cry, he hugged me.

"What is she talking about?" I cried.

"Shhh, try to calm down. I don't know." He rubbed my back. "Just try to calm down. I'll get the boys to take you back to your grandparents'."

"That won't be necessary," I looked up to see another officer say. "Her grandparents are here to get her."

He said grandparents. That meant both of them were here. I was supposed to be back before Jacob got home, and I wasn't. I wondered if my grandmother covered for me, and if she didn't, how much trouble would I be in? I could still feel the sting on my cheek from where Jacob had slapped me at the dinner table.

I was escorted to the waiting area, but it wasn't Jacob or Henrietta waiting for me. It was my mother's parents. Shock didn't describe the intensity of how I was feeling. I hadn't seen them in years. Did Jerome's parents know they were there to get me? And where were they? Surely, they had heard about it all by now.

I stared at Gran and Gramps numbly. I vaguely remembered them—younger, less wrinkles and grayed hair—but the features of who they were still distinct in my memories. I wasn't leaving with them. I'd rather go back to the prison that was the Bonovich estate before I went with those who were now complete strangers to me.

I could feel the eyes of my friends on me, watching this part of my literal hell unfold. My eyes diverted to Toby who I could sense was about to make a move before I even saw the determination on his face. One wrong word or move and he'd come to my rescue—I had no doubt.

"Jorja," Gran said, with a few steps forward.

Gramps looked apologetic and sincere, but he could save it. I didn't need that from him.

"I'm not going anywhere with either of you," I said, taking a step back.

Toby came over, standing protectively at my side. A few seconds later, Rush was at my other side. I watched as all of my friends stood.

"She is currently in the custody of Jacob and Henrietta Bonovich," Officer True said to the officer. His name tag said Bryant, and he must have been new because I had never seen him in Grove before. He turned his attention to my mother's parents. "I can't let her go with you. I'm sorry Officer Bryant led you to believe otherwise."

I looked at Officer True, hoping he understood my pleading eyes to get me out of there. I could feel the oppression of everything settling into my bones. Any moment, I was going to break, and I couldn't stand to be stared at like this by everyone a second longer.

"Boys, take her to my office," he said to Rush and Toby.

I felt their hands on my back, carefully urging me to start walking. Officer True opened the locked door once again and allowed us through. Toby and Rush escorted me to his office, shutting and locking the door behind them.

And that was the moment I lost it. If there were papers, I tossed them, chairs were thrown, pens scattered the floor. By the time my efforts to destroy everything in sight were exhausted, I slammed my back against the wall and slid down until I was seated on the floor. I hugged my knees to my chest and buried my face against them. I could hear Toby and Rush cleaning up the mess. Part of me wanted to help them, but I was too tired.

The weight of it all came crashing down.

Brian's death.

The possibility that Jerome wasn't dead.

Someone who was or looked like Jerome tried to kill me and was still out there.

My mother saying the things she did.

Peter and Olivia forming an alliance.

My real father fighting for custody. A battle he most likely would lose.

The irresistible urge to take the entire Bonovich empire down consumed me more than ever before. A thirst for it that couldn't be quenched. It was all-consuming, gnawing at my every waking moment—even stronger now. A ravenous beast, pushing forward to take down every sinister operation, every corrupt connection and wicked deed. It was a flame that would never dim, the only thing keeping me afloat and moving forward. The promise of justice gave a glimmer of hope for a new beginning. This thirst for redemption was a fight for the future. *My* future.

CHAPTER THIRTY-FIVE

Rush

"What are we doing here?" I asked in a hushed tone as Toby fidgeted with Dad's work keys at the back door of the police station. "They're going to notice us here." I looked over my shoulder. Toby told me to come with him, but he didn't tell me exactly what we were doing.

"I'm getting something for Jorja." The mention of her name coming from his mouth made me tense. I saw what was happening between them right before my eyes. I knew what it was, but I struggled to admit it. He opened the door. "Be quiet, and move quickly."

I followed him down the back hallway. Jorja's mom was bailed out by her parents last I heard, so she wouldn't be there now. Toby was convinced the officers on call were in their offices and the dispatcher was at the front. I had hoped he was right.

And he was wrong.

He darted into a nearby closet, pulling me in with him. He shut the door quickly but quietly.

"Can you tell me what we're here for?" I whispered.

"The metal box Jorja's mom had."

"Of course that's what we're getting." I groaned. "Do you even know if it's still here? I'm sure it's being analyzed by some really smart detective."

"I'm here to find out."

He cracked the door open then whispered, "It's clear now. Let's go."

We hurried out and down the hallway. Toby stopped at the door where they locked up the evidence. I kept watch while he tried each key. He got it open just as someone started down the hall, and I pushed him inside, whispering, *"Go, go, go!"*

I shut the door behind us as quietly as I could and locked it. The footsteps down the hall got louder as they came closer. Toby and I stood still in the dark room, holding our breath to not make a sound.

The footsteps stopped right by the door.

"Hide," Toby whispered.

We scrambled to find a hiding spot and settled behind a large shelf. The smell of weed filled the air. The door opened, and when the light came on, I saw we were hiding behind a shelf of confiscated drugs.

We remained crouched down but ready to run if needed. There were two men in the room, and they weren't dressed in uniforms. Instead, they were dressed in all black, concealing their faces with black masks. This was some stuff straight out of a movie I didn't want to be in.

They started tearing through everything obviously looking for something specific. In my gut, I knew what they were there for. They wanted what we wanted. Toby tapped my shoulder and pointed to my right. The box was right there, sitting on the bottom shelf where firearms were labeled in cases. I shook my head. The best thing we could do was sit there until they left.

He stared at me, the look of determination filled his eyes, and I knew he wasn't leaving without that damn box.

"It's silver with a combination lock," a gruff voice said from behind one of the masks.

"We need to hurry before someone realizes the entire staff here tonight is dead," the second masked guy said.

Dead. He said dead.

I was relieved Dad was at home, but panic filled me that everyone else was dead. Toby had tunnel vision. His eyes remained on the box. I felt like I was going to throw up. We needed to get out of there. They could have the damn box.

Before I could try to stop him, Toby was quietly hurrying over to the box. He grabbed it, accidentally knocking off a case that held a firearm. The men turned in a hurry, just as Toby yelled, "RUN!"

We ran out of the room as fast as we could; the sound of heavy footsteps traveling quickly behind us made me move faster. We went out the back door, a gunshot grazed past my face, the burning sensation of it barely touching my left ear made my heart pound faster. I didn't have time to process the near-death experience. We made it to Toby's truck and sped off.

He tossed the box into my lap. "Hold on!"

"Are they following us?" I asked, before looking in the window confirming that they were. "Shit. Shit. Shit." I closed my eyes.

"Call Dad!"

I set the box on the floorboard between my feet and got out my phone. My hands shook so badly it was hard to pull up his contact to call. Everything felt like it was moving in slow motion. I put the phone to my ear.

"Hello?" Dad answered sleepily.

"We're being followed! They killed everyone at the station!" I looked over my shoulder. "We got the box, but they wanted it. This is Toby's fault!"

"What!" Dad hollered, fully awake now. "Where are you?

"Toby's driving. I don't know. We're—" My words were cut off when the truck was struck from Toby's side, and we flipped several times.

I was in and out of consciousness, gasping for air. Everything went completely still, the sound of a liquid spraying and smoke filled the space around us.

"Toby," I struggled to say.

He didn't answer.

I heard the screech of tires before the vehicle hit us again, sending us flipping downward until what was left of the truck submerged into the water.

The river.

The river that ran the edge of Grove where we dumped the body. How fucking ironic to die there.

I closed my eyes, unable to move. I closed my eyes and held my breath, and the darkness consumed me.

CHAPTER THIRTY-SIX

Toby

I woke, gasping for air, completely drenched and freezing in the embrace of water. We were sinking. My body thrashed in disorientation as the water came in fast from all sides. Panic set in, surging through my veins, as the entirety of the situation filled my mind.

Rush!

My brother's name echoed in my mind like a prayer, pleading with God and the universe to not let him die. He was unconscious, and the water was coming in faster. My hands pushed against the window, but as fast as the water was coming in, there was no time to try to break it or to save Rush.

"Rush," I screamed, my voice silenced in the flood of water.

Desperately, I reached over to try to shake Rush, but the force of the water made it impossible to move. I found his wrist and held onto it, my muscles straining against the crushing weight of the water. The truck was sinking fast and the suffocating pressure inside the cab made my lungs burn for air. No matter how hard I fought, the water was unyielding and pulling us deeper.

The darkness claimed us, and as my consciousness slipped away, bright lights filled the surface of the water. I could feel myself being pulled from the water and worried voices surrounded me but they all blurred together until it they faded into nothing.

CHAPTER THIRTY-SEVEN

Jorja

Have you ever felt fully alive but were convinced you were actually dead and all of the events unfolding before you were just a figment of your imagination— a nightmare on repeat from the demons manipulating your brain?

How sadistic was fate that the night the two people I cared about the most were found dying in the same water Jerome's body was also found—if it was his body at all. Was this a joke? Or some form of karma bestowed upon me by the demons Jerome or his possible twin met in hell?

I looked down at Becca's hand holding mine. My best friend was the only thing keeping me grounded and sane. When she came to the house, waking me up screaming that Toby and Rush were in an accident, the moments that followed blurred together, feeling like my own personal death. I was moving, but slowly dying.

"Jorja, breathe," Becca reminded me. She had been saying that every few minutes.

I looked at her, blinking a few times. I looked around the room at my friends. Tommy had his head in his hands, left leg bouncing nervously. Beck had his head resting against the wall and hat over his face to hide his tears. He hated crying in front of people. Wren and Jena whispered quietly to each other, tears clinging to their own cheeks.

How did this even happen?

Where were they?

Was this caused by the same person who shot me?

I felt like I was going to be sick. I jumped from my chair and hurried outside—all of the contents from my stomach splattered the front lawn of the hospital entrance. I could hear Becca telling someone to get napkins, then she grabbed my hair to hold it back as I got sick again. I fell to my knees and gripped the grass in my hands.

"Is she okay?" I heard Officer True's tired voice ask.

Becca handed me some paper towels. "No, she's not."

After cleaning my face, I stood. Officer True handed me a bottle of water.

"Thank you," I said weakly. "Any updates?"

"They're both going to be fine. They're very lucky." He looked over his shoulder at all of my friends. "I need to talk to her alone. Can you all head back inside?"

No one argued, although I could tell Becca wanted to. Once they were gone and we were alone, he looked at me, his eyes narrowing into a fiery glare.

"This all stops now," he said sternly. "All of it. Do you know why my boys almost died tonight?"

I shook my head. "No, sir."

"Because Toby went after the box. The box you said you wanted. You stay away from my boys. Do you hear me? You're ruining their life!"

The weight of his words knocked me down. It killed me because I knew I couldn't argue with him. He was right.

A few tears trickled down my cheeks. "I'm—"

"Don't you dare say sorry. You knew what you were doing. You knew! Go to your grandparents'. Stay away from Rush and Toby. If you don't, I will tell everyone who killed Jerome. I will tell the whole fucking world and will make sure you rot in hell with every single Bonovich."

As he walked away, I stood there, frozen still in the wake of his words. The distance between us grew larger and larger until he was inside the hospital.

Everything felt far away. The world kept spinning as I just stood there staring at the hospital doors, feeling more lost than ever before. Officer True just pulled the plug of the only thing keeping me alive.

"Jorja," I heard Mr. Bill say from behind me. His voice sounded muffled, though it wasn't. The air that surrounded me was thick with regrets and pain.

I turned to look at him, confused as to how I was even still standing. My legs felt like Jell-O.

Breathe in.

Breathe out.

I repeated that to myself, fully aware of every single breath I took, which made it harder to breathe.

"Jorja," he repeated. "I was coming to see if you were ready to leave when I saw you standing here." He frowned. "Are you alright? Are your friends going to be okay?"

"Take me to my mother."

Her parents had bailed her out, and she was staying with them on house arrest while under investigation for the fire.

"I don't think that's a good—"

"I'm not asking, Mr. Bill. If you don't, I will find a way, and you know that."

He sighed heavily. "Your grandmother won't be happy."

"She doesn't have a say."

He nodded. "Alright, let's go, but if she asks or your grandfather asks, we never left the hospital."

When we arrived at my mother's parents' house, the SUV Mr. Bill was driving had barely come to a stop and I was getting out. I stormed my way to the front door and started pounding my fist against it. When Gran opened the door, I moved past her and into the house.

"Where is she?" I yelled.

"Jorja, stop it right now!" Gran shouted.

"What's going on?" Gramps asked as he walked into the living room.

I made my way down the hall opening every single door until I found her in a bedroom sitting on the bed. I was pretty sure Gran and Gramps were following me, but I didn't stop to look.

"What's in the box?" I screamed.

She stood and moved slowly toward the mirror as if she were drugged. She didn't answer, she just stared at herself in the mirror. Her silence only fueled my anger more. I grabbed her by the shoulders, shaking her.

"Tell me what's in the box!"

She didn't try to make me stop, she just stared at me. Forceful sobs escaped me as Mr. Bill and Gramps pulled me away from her. I screamed at her, begging her to tell me. Begging her to fix this somehow. I knew she could. She had to know the answers to everything. She *had* to.

I was pulled into the living room and forced to sit on the couch.

"You have to calm down," Gramps shouted as he and Mr. Bill held me still on the couch.

"Let me go!" I begged. I cried until I couldn't anymore. Exhaustion filled me, and I finally relaxed, causing them to finally let go.

"Your mother is in a state of shock right now. Since they found Jerome's body, they are requesting her to come view it. She was hysterical and had to be medicated."

"Toby and Rush almost died tonight because of that box. Because of her." A few tears trickled down my cheeks, and I wondered how I had any tears left at all.

"Those boys had no business getting involved with anything your mother has a part of. None of you do," Gran said calmly. "Not even your mother. She chose this life, and now she's dealing with the consequences. You are all children who have no business involving yourselves in such dangerous affairs."

That confirmed that Gran and Gramps knew some of what the Bonoviches were up to. Maybe it was a new revelation for them and Mom told them everything, or maybe they had always known. None of that mattered, though. All that mattered now was finding out the truth about everything.

The pain of Officer True's words hit me again in a wave of searing torture. He couldn't have meant it. He couldn't take them away from me. This wasn't how any of this was supposed to go. I did tell Toby I had to get that box, but I never asked him or Rush to do it. I told them not to get involved with me. I should've ghosted them both. I dragged them into this mess. I allowed them in and let down walls I shouldn't have. I allowed them to see me, to fall for me. I allowed my heart to fall for them, too. I was a villain in this story and would openly admit that. But I'd make it right somehow. This was just another chess piece in the game—a move forward.

Mr. Bill said my name, gaining my attention. "Let's get you back to your grandparents' house. You need to rest."

I needed to be with Rush and Toby. I needed to know they were okay and see it for myself that they were breathing and alive. But what I needed and what would be allowed didn't line up, so I had to settle for Mr. Bill's suggestion. For now, anyway.

I nodded and stood slowly.

I looked at Gran. "When does she go view the body to confirm it's him?"

"In the morning," she answered solemnly.

"I want to go."

"I don't think that's—"

Mr. Bill cut her off. "That's not your decision to make. The ones who hold custody of her right now will make that decision."

I wondered if Jacob or Henrietta would allow it.

I wanted to put my eyes on the man I murdered and make sure it was the right one.

CHAPTER THIRTY-EIGHT

Rush

I sat up slowly because moving too quickly was a mistake I made earlier. I looked to my right and saw Toby in bed asleep. I moved my hand and was reminded there was an IV in it when the tubing got caught on the armrest of the hospital bed. My skin felt like tiny needles were stabbing it over and over. My chest felt tight. I started coughing and couldn't stop.

Dad hurried to my side, and that was when I realized he was in the room.

My chest burned as I struggled to catch my breath.

Once the coughing stopped, Dad handed me a cup of water, and I took a few slow sips. I was surprised I didn't wake Toby up.

I handed Dad the cup. "Thank you," I barely got out. My voice was strained, and every word made my head pound.

"The doctor said you'd be like this for a while. How are you feeling?"

"Tired." I looked over at Toby again. "How is he?" I asked, speaking slowly.

I tried to remember everything how it happened, but things just weren't coming in clear at all.

"Lucky to be alive. Both of you are. The doctor is shocked that you both made it out alive and nothing broken. It's a miracle."

"Everything hurts."

He nodded. "And it will for a while."

I wondered if Jorja ever showed up. Tommy, Beck, Wren, Becca, and Jena were all there. They came in to see me, but I was so out of it I couldn't talk. I never saw Jorja, though, and was too tired to form the words to ask where she was.

The thought of the guys we were running from saying they killed everyone in the police station resurfaced in my mind.

I looked at Dad. "The police station."

His jaw tensed.

"Your friends. Your coworkers. They were killed."

He nodded slowly. "Yes."

I laid my head against the pillow and closed my eyes. "Did you find the box?"

"We found more than the box."

I looked at him.

He cleared his throat and sat in the chair next to the bed. "We found Jerome's body. With the impact of the truck into the water, it must've stirred up what was on the bottom and with the river being lower than normal, it was there in plain sight."

"Does Jorja know?"

"I'm not sure."

My eyes narrowed. "Was she not here?"

"She was."

"And?

He looked at his watch, obviously stalling.

"Dad."

He looked at me. "I told her to leave. I was angry. I don't want her near you two anymore."

If I had had the strength to argue with him, I would have, but my eyes were so heavy, and I started drifting off to sleep again no matter how hard I tried to fight it.

After three days of being in the hospital for observation, we were finally home. Dad hadn't told Toby about him banning Jorja from us since he was worse off and going to take longer to recover physically from all of this. He didn't want to add stress to an already stressful situation, but ... I let it slip. Toby was starting to ask questions about why she hadn't been by to see us or why she wasn't responding to text messages. My guilt got the best of me. I couldn't stand to see him suffer, and I was sick of suffering in silence. I broke.

"You can't leave," I said as I slowly stood from the couch. Every inch of my body still ached.

Toby struggled to put on his shoes. His bruised ribs made it hard for him to bend over. After tying the laces, he stood. "I think we're past anyone telling me what to do."

"Dad will be home soon. Look, I'm all for going to see her too, but let's just wait this out. Dad will come around. We could've died, Toby. It makes sense why he'd be angry with her. He'll calm down."

"I'm not waiting for him to calm down. When everyone was here visiting us earlier, Becca let it slip that Jorja was going to view the body in the morning. I have to talk to her."

"Why?"

He shook his head. "I just do. If Dad comes home, tell him where I am. This is bigger than him wanting us to stay away from her. I can't stay away from her. I won't. In two months, we will be eighteen, and he won't be able to stop me."

"I'll go with you."

He shook his head again. "No." He took his jacket off the hook near the door. "I'm doing this alone."

I wanted to see her, too, but Toby was making it abundantly clear he wanted to see her alone. I could ask questions all day long, but if he didn't want to tell me, he wouldn't. Him and I were different like that. He was fine suffering in silence.

"Do you even know where she is?"

"Becca told me she's at her grandparents' mansion." I watched as he grabbed the keys to my truck.

I sighed heavily as I sat back down. "And what if those people who were chasing us are still looking for us?"

He shrugged. "I'm sure they already know where to find us."

I knew nothing I said would stop him. "Be careful."

"I'll try to be back before Dad gets home."

I watched as he walked out to the door.

Even with everything going on, I couldn't shake the feeling of jealousy. I was losing Jorja, and I knew it. Toby and her had this undeniable bond that almost didn't make sense, but it worked. Part of me hated him for it because if he never let down his walls for her, I'd be the one she wanted. I almost had her, but she slipped through my fingertips, a slow and painful release that made it harder to breathe than almost drowning.

CHAPTER THIRTY-NINE

Jorja

I was almost asleep when I heard my bedroom door open and close quietly. Panic filled me, my heart feeling like it'd beat right out of my chest. No one came into my room without a knock. I laid there, concentrating on keeping my breathing slow and quiet.

Why didn't I keep a gun under my pillow?

"Jorja," Toby's whisper instantly calmed me.

I sat up in bed quickly, almost crying as I got out of bed and flung myself into his arms.

His entire body tensed, and the low grunt reminded me that he was still in a lot of pain from the accident. I tried to move away, but his arms wrapped tighter around me.

"No, stay right here," he begged quietly.

"Toby, you're shaking."

"I don't care," he whispered, laying his head on top of mine.

"How'd you get in here?"

"Your grandmother."

I hated the way his body trembled. I moved back and took his hand in mine. We walked over to my bed and sat down. I held onto his hand tightly.

"You weren't responding to my texts." Was Toby crying? A tear falling down his cheek confirmed he was.

"Your dad told me not to."

He nodded slowly. "I need to tell you something before you view the body tomorrow."

"How'd you—"

"Becca told me." The dim light from the moon shining through the balcony doors illuminated his face as he looked at me. "I shot Jerome."

My eyes widened. "What?"

"The day he killed her, and Rush told me he saw him ... I ... I got one of my dad's guns, and I hid in the graveyard by the funeral home. I watched him for an entire week to figure out where he would be and when so I could make my move. I noticed he was making runs to the funeral home late at night. So, one night, as he was getting out of his car, I shot him in the right shoulder. Someone was with him, but I never saw them. They were in the car, got out in a hurry, and I took off into the woods surrounding the graveyard. He'll have a bullet wound in the right shoulder. That's if you can even recognize him at all. The water probably has made him unrecognizable. But it'll confirm if it's him or if our suspicions of him being a twin is true."

"The mortician at our funeral home said that whoever wrapped him in the trash bag did a good job because barely any water went through. His body, according to them, is actually mostly recognizable. For legal purposes, my mother has to view it, and I demanded to go. I can't look for that bullet wound with everyone there."

"Then let's go now."

"Toby, you're hurt. People that work for Jerome and Jacob are watching more closely now. None of us are safe. Your dad is right, you need to stay away from me."

He shook his head as more tears fell down his cheeks. "I can't do that."

Tears filled my own eyes. "Being together feels like a gun pointed right at us. This isn't safe. It's reckless. Toby, you have to go back home. I almost lost you and Rush. I can't keep doing this. Putting everyone in danger for myself is unfair. I don't want to be this person."

"If you don't go with me, then I'm going myself. I need to know if it's him."

The determination in his eyes and voice told me he wasn't backing down. "Okay. Let's go." I wouldn't let him go alone.

I went to the bathroom to change out of my pajamas and into a pair of black leggings and black hoodie. This was stupid and extremely dangerous, but knowing he'd go without me no matter what I said scared me worse than going with him.

After putting on shoes, he and I quietly made our way through the house—careful not to get caught while sneaking through the garage—grabbed the key to the funeral home Jacob kept with all the other keys, and hurried out to his truck. I got into the passenger side and watched as he got in and cranked the engine.

As he drove down the road, he held my hand, pulling me to the middle. Once I was seated right next to him, he put his arm around my waist and kept me close. Neither of us spoke—what was there to say? We would probably die tonight, and though we were fully aware of that revelation, we still went despite the fact our final breaths were most likely near.

"Park at the gas station, and we'll walk the rest of the way," I suggested, and he pulled into the small gas station that was closed for the night.

We got out of the truck and hurried through the trees that lined the highway. I kept the funeral home key clutched in my hand, careful not to drop it. Panic filled me but also fueled each step, urging me to run faster. I didn't know how Toby was keeping up, but he never slowed down.

When we made it to the funeral home, I struggled to unlock the back door with the way my hands were shaking. Toby took the key from me and opened it. He stuck the key in the pocket of his jeans, and we hurried inside. I went to the alarm system to turn it off, but someone had changed the code.

"It's not working!" I tried several more times, cursing.

When the alarm sounded, Toby took my hand, and yelled, "We have to hurry!"

I kept his hand in mine as we ran faster downstairs to the morgue. We started opening the drawers to the freezers that preserved the bodies until we found Jerome's. The mortician was right. The body was swollen but the flesh wasn't affected by saponification, a process I'd seen when helping in the morgue of bodies that had drowned and weren't recovered for weeks.

"We are going to have to lift him over together," I said quickly and loud enough for him to hear me over the alarm.

On the count of three we lifted his right side enough to see his shoulder.

No bullet wound.

It wasn't Jerome.

"We have to go," I said, my voice shaking with the realization that I killed the wrong man. That Jerome Bonovich most definitely had a twin, and how good of an actor his twin was, making me think it was Jerome.

Just as Toby and I laid him back down and shut the drawer, his dad and several other officers came running into the room, demanding we put our hands in the air. Toby and I followed their request, and when his dad realized it was us, he lowered his gun and demanded the other officers did the same.

To be continued...

Acknowledgements

To my BETA Readers. How do I even form words to express how much I appreciate you all? Your dedication and passion for my work has truly brought my words to life. You have kept me accountable and excited to move forward when I felt stuck.

To Nora Blake's Street Team. Although we just started, I cannot wait to see where the future takes us in the book world. You are *my* people and I will forever be grateful the universe saw fit to bring us together.

To the Memphis Girls Book Club, honestly, I have Taylor Swift to thank for bringing us together. If it weren't for my Swiftie-heart, I would've never met Reagan. I'm extremely thankful for your discussions, honest opinions, and the warm welcome you gave my book. You are all rock stars, and I'm forever thankful for each of you!

A *huge* thank you to my editor, Wendi. Even when I'm cursing you when I'm eliminating the billion "I"s you detected, I still love you and your ability to be brutally honest because you know the quality of the book comes before my feelings.

Lastly, to my readers: you are the reason I write. Your love for my stories, your kind words, and your support mean the world to me. Thank you for embarking on this journey with me. Your encouragement keeps me inspired every single day.

Nora B.